Don't Get Mad Get Even

Colin Goodwin

PUBLISHING

First Edition published 2015 by
2QT Limited (Publishing)
Settle, North Yorkshire BD24 9RH United Kingdom

This is a work of fiction and any resemblance to any person
living or dead is purely coincidental. The place names
mentioned are real but have no connection with the events in
this book.

Cover Design by Charlotte Mouncey

Printed in Great Britain by Lightning Source UK Ltd

A CIP catalogue record for this book is available
from the British Library
ISBN 978-1-910077-60-3

Don't
Get Mad
Get Even

April, Throttle Village:
The Cricket and the Shenanigans Begin

'Brainless gits,' muttered Albert Bradley as rust and muck stuck to the sweat on his forehead.

He was removing the closed season's cobwebs and rust from some metal frames when a small group of people, all hunched together, made their way past his house and up to the cricket pavilion opposite. Albert knew them immediately; they were hardly recognisable in the fading light but, although they were within nodding distance, pleasantries were not exchanged. In fact, he purposefully turned away and snarled as he wire-brushed.

For most people the lighter nights and budding plants provide a feeling of renewal, a spirit of optimism with summer just around the corner, but for Albert, April had other implications. His annual ritual had begun in earnest and so, donning a well-used boiler suit, old gardening gloves and his third-best flat cap, he dragged out two metal-framed mesh panels from his garage. He leaned them against the fence and pondered the awful job of getting them clean enough to grace the front of his house.

'What's the point of having a smart house if you have to put these sodding things on it for six months?' he grunted.

His front garden used to be his pride and joy. He had won many trophies for his dahlias and roses at the local village fêtes and once thought about going to the county show for the bigger prizes, but events beyond his control had put a stop to that. The up-and-coming cricketers appeared to be dosed with the same growth fertilizer that he used. Unfortunately, the result was that the players had outgrown the size of the pitch. These tall, hefty lads could slog the ball with ease up to the front of his house.

Albert cleaned one side of a panel then threw down the brush in frustration. 'Got to sort this once and for all,' he ranted, spitting out old bits of paint and getting angrier.

He had come up with all manner of guards to protect his prize flower heads from the ball but after several direct hits, many near misses and numerous arguments he considered it futile to carry on. So, after one such incident, he had his lovingly nurtured strip of land paved over. Being an occasion too distressing for him to witness, he stayed out of sight; as the workmen piled his nurtured plants into the skip and tamped down the concrete slabs, he sat in the kitchen, hands firmly clasped around his favourite mug, and scowled.

His wife, initially a supportive soul who more recently had come close to either braining him with a heavy object or just walking out, was fully aware of his condition. She silently and dutifully provided sweet tea to guard against the shock of the occasion but, as he irritatingly slurped the tea through his teeth, they both knew that it would take more than three heaped spoonfuls of sugar to offset the bitterness and resentment building up inside him.

Throttle Cricket Club:
An Emergency Meeting

In the fading light, the silhouette of Throttle Cricket Club pavilion was quite imposing. Its large clock face high up in the eaves provided an appearance of significance in the sporting world. Unfortunately, the clock was irreparably broken. Clattered by a direct hit two seasons before by a member of the opposite side, the clock now permanently displayed twenty-past five. The other deception was that of the apparent solid grandeur of its fifties design; the pavilion was actually a crumbling wreck. The mainly wooden structure had been left to the elements for as long as anyone could remember; in daylight, the wood rot and peeling paint were obvious. Some locals said it made them feel at home, so the building developed into what it is now: a structure held together with string and rusty nails, where the doors were closed gently, not slammed, and no one dared open a window in case it fell out.

The assembled committee sat down, not knowing the reason for the hastily arranged meeting. John Appleby, the club chairman, had presided over many such meetings and had a well-practised stance. His fat neck blended into the contours of his bloated belly where his trouser belt appeared to be strangling his waist. As he coughed and cleared his throat, the threads of his waistcoat buttons stretched to the limit. Then, when all was silent, he peered over the half-moon glasses perched on the end of his nose and apologised sombrely.

'Sorry to drag you here on a miserably cold night but summat's cropped up. I got this, this morning from Sir Alfred T. Bullock and Son. Thought I'd better bring it to your attention before somebody else does.' He waved the single sheet of paper in the air to prove its existence.

'Better be urgent. This is my pool night up the shoot if it drags on,' moaned Tom the groundsman, whose ruddy complexion confirmed that he had spent years facing the biting easterly wind and who was niggled at being dragged back after spending the whole day repairing the fence at the ground.

The chairman stared at him. 'The sooner there's order, the sooner you find out, OK?' he replied, raising his voice.

After a moment's silence, he tilted his head back and focused on the letter. 'Here we go then, from Sir Alfred T. Bullock and Son. "I have to inform you and the members of Throttle Cricket Club that, as laid down in the tenants' agreement, within any ten-year period you have to win a trophy. No trophy or cup has been won for nine years. Therefore, you have only one season left to comply with this rule. After that time, the use of the ground will be returned to the estate of Sir Alfred T Bullock and Son. Yours, Roland Bullock."'

Committee meetings had always been lively affairs with banter flowing, but on this occasion total silence shrouded the members like an invisible blanket and took away their ability to speak. Mouths dropped open but nothing came forth.

Tom, never short of a word for too long, blurted out, 'The scheming git wants to build on it, that's all it can be. Anyway, how come we didn't know this time bomb was ticking away?'

Heads turned to face Arthur, the secretary. 'Don't look at me,' he defended himself. 'I don't look at the frigging deeds from one year t' next. Besides, I have only been here for five years. How the hell am I supposed to know what went on in '96?'

'Must be worth a fortune,' added Fred the treasurer quietly, whilst scribbling on a pad.

The others turned his way.

'Why?' asked Janice, all-round help, or as she called it, 'dogsbody'.

'The ground, smack in the middle of the village, it's prime building land to a speculator. Hundred houses on there, each worth two hundred grand, worth a fortune.'

The committee members looked depressed.

'Well, thanks for that cheery note. Point is, what the hell are we going to do about it?' appealed Arthur.

'We'll start by keeping calm,' advised Tom as he took a final swig to finish his pint. He shuddered as the beer hit the spot, then announced, 'Then we'll do what we always do in a crisis.'

He paused and looked around as they waited for words of wisdom. 'We'll organise another frigging meeting.' He rose and pushed back his chair.

The noise of the chair legs scraping the floor indicated his intention to leave. As a parting shot, he stared at the chairman.

'Do it, John, but this time make it a big one, all invited, then there's no secrets. Everyone will know what the scheming Bullocks are up to, OK?'

Then he held his stomach, grimaced, and belched loudly. 'Crap ale and that heater stinks,' he muttered as he left the building.

The others turned to look at an old bottled gas heater in its rusty casing. The yellow sooty flame that gave off little heat indicated that it was well past its best.

'Can you smell gas?' pondered Janice to the others.

The Bullock Household:
A Frosty Breakfast

The Bullocks' house, as the locals referred to it, was a tall, detached Victorian dwelling perched on a raised plateau of land overlooking the village of Throttle. Its multifaceted roof clearly indicated that beneath was a maze of rooms sufficient to house a very large family and, in times past, butlers and house cleaners. Instead, it housed one couple and their son.

The breakfast arrangements at the Bullock household had deteriorated into a simple format.

Sir Alfred T. Bullock, wheelchair-bound since falling from a ladder, was arguing with his son Roland as usual. Since his father's accident, Roland had taken over the day-to-day running of the firm, but it was not to his father's liking.

'You've done what?' yelled Sir Alf, spitting half the contents of his mouth across the table.

'I've sent the cricket club what is in effect notice to quit,' replied Roland casually. With a smirk guaranteed to wind his father up even further, he went on, 'It's quite legal, I've looked it up in the deeds. If they don't win a cup, and they won't, the land comes back to us. Easy,' he said smugly.

'The land, the land, we don't need the bleeding land! It was my decision to give them the land in the first place, so it'll be my say-so when we want it back, OK?' Sir Alf emphasised his point by banging the table and in the process upsetting most of the coffee cups.

'Too late, the letter's gone. Oh, and by the way, if you recall, you gave me the authority to make decisions when you put me in charge. Or have you conveniently forgotten that?' Roland pointed defiantly.

Lady Miriam Bullock, sitting at the other end of the long table, nibbled her toast whilst watching the back and forth of the argument. As she watched, her face displayed her anger.

'That's it, I'm off. I can't stand this bloody bickering. It's pathetic the way you two carry on. I've had enough of your antics. From now on I'm skipping breakfast.' She pushed away her bowl of muesli, tipping over the last remaining upright coffee cup in the process.

Miriam had dropped the 'Lady' prefix ages ago on the basis that it seemed a mite pretentious where outside toilets and coal sheds still existed in the village. She had seen the relationship between her husband and son deteriorate from at best frosty silences to at worst slanging matches just short of violence. To add to this, she had to witness the steady destruction of her dream home. Once she could boast about the designer interior and country roses round the door; now, the home that had been shortlisted for an article in a glossy county magazine was being progressively wrecked by the ramps and lifts installed to accommodate her husband's wheelchair. Miriam had been reduced to tears as the extortionately priced wallpaper and the artistically scumbled doors and skirting succumbed to the treatment meted out by Alf's careless driving.

'I see you've smashed another doorway. I'll be glad when you're bedridden and out of the way,' she growled heartlessly.

'Sorry, love, this new one's tekking some getting used to. Mind of its own,' Alf explained, gazing at the controls.

'Don't call me love, you know it grates on me. Anyway, the only thing you ever loved was your soddin' mill.' Sir Alf looked up as Miriam's eyes tightened with hatred. 'Funny really. Love life gone, mill nearly gone, you wrecking this place quicker than we can repair it... well I'm going too.' And with that, she slammed the door behind her so hard it rattled the plates in an adjacent cupboard.

'Ungrateful bitch!' he shouted. He stared at the door for a moment then turned to Roland. 'As for you, cancel that soddin' letter.'

There was a pause as Sir Alf's brain ruminated over Miriam's parting shot. 'What does she mean about the mill being gone? Gone where?'

Roland stood up and backed away from the table. 'The letter's gone out, last week as a matter of fact, and the mill's not going anywhere. Look, got to go,' he said hastily as he shut the door with a little less force than his mother had.

Suddenly all was still. Alf sat in his wheelchair staring at the mess that was the breakfast table until a voice from behind reminded him that he was not entirely alone.

'Finished, 'ave you, sir?' enquired Flora, the daily help, with a familiarity that made him smile.

In a split second, hearing that voice had changed him from sad and miserable to a person who believed that the day had more to offer. He observed Flora retrieving a fork that had fallen to the floor.

'You all right?' she queried as she pulled at the edge of her skirt.

'Improving,' he replied.

The Perkins' House:
A New Future?

Geoffrey and Susan Perkins and their daughter Alison had recently moved to Throttle village with the promise of a new life provided from the earnings of his new job as sales and marketing manager for the local Old Goat Brewery.

'You'll love it up here, the rugged landscape and fresh northern air, plus we get a lot more house for our money,' he preached.

'Shops,' Susan said when they were looking around the village. 'Where are the shops? I've spotted a chippy, a pub and a paper shop. Where are the proper shops? Or do I have to walk around in rags like the rest of them?'

'A bus ride away. You'll see, as soon as you get to know the place,' he lied. He was getting used to lying; he found it easier than explaining.

Later, Geoffrey was standing on the doorstep surveying all he owned or as Susan corrected him, 'All that the bank owns,' when he heard a curious scraping noise accompanied by cussing and swearing. He walked across the grass and peered over the fence.

'Nice night,' he said hastily as his new neighbour, Albert Bradley, turned and spotted him.

Albert looked up from his labours. Specks of rust had stuck to the sweat on his brow and the red dust mixed with raindrops on his glasses amplified the anger in his eyes.

'Nice night, nice sodding night?' he repeated, spitting bits of rust and waving the scraper as he spoke. 'I'm scraping the shit off these, it's starting to chuck it down, and you call it a nice night.'

Shocked at the response, Geoffrey stepped back from the fence. 'Sorry, didn't mean to be nosy. Just wondered what you were doing.'

'You've a set of these, you know, back of your garage. Better get yours painted and fitted or your house will look like a knackered old pepper pot,' Albert advised with an air of manic cleverness that disturbed Geoffrey.

They went into Geoffrey's garage and Albert pointed towards four frames.

'I wondered what they were for,' said Geoffrey, still puzzled as to their use.

'See,' said Albert, pulling a cobweb-encrusted frame from the wall.

'What do they do?' Geoffrey asked anxiously.

'They stop the ball coming through the window,' said Albert grinning.

A voice from behind casually asked, 'What ball, whose window?'

They turned to see Susan standing in the driveway.

'Oh nothing, love,' said Geoffrey, trying to fend off a row, but he failed.

'Cricket club's ball, through your window,' said Albert, smirking. 'You must have noticed you are right in the firing line. From your living-room window, you can look right down the batsman's throat,' he added, opening his mouth wide and pointing with his finger for effect.

'They'd never reach here … would they?' Geoffrey asked.

Ten minutes later in the kitchen, Susan ranted, 'You stupid, idiotic fool! Nice to have a house near a village cricket pitch, you said. Turns out we are living on the bloody pitch, prisoners in our own home on Saturdays. Our Alison will be killed instantly if she gets hit.'

'Sundays and Wednesdays too,' Geoffrey muttered quietly.

'We'll never be able to sell this house. No wonder he was keen to lower the price and give us the carpets,' she went on. 'That estate agent, he must have known, the devious git. I remember him being pushy, saying we had a bargain.'

Geoffrey stood and listened.

'My mother comes on Saturday afternoons, what about her? She will have to come in the back way; she will never believe this when I tell her. This is all your fault.' Susan stared at him in a fit of rage. 'You absolute imbecile... what are you wittering about?'

'I've seen the fixture list, they play on Saturdays, Sundays and Wednesdays too,' Geoffrey said meekly.

Without hesitation, she threw the contents of the mug she was holding at him. He stood, motionless and dripping, as she strutted past him. Their daughter Alison, who had been listening at the door, approached him. 'Daddy,' she said softly.

'Yes, love, what is it?' he replied, mopping his face with a piece of kitchen roll.

'What's an imbecile?'

Throttle World Press:
Nasty Goings On

Arnold Bosworth, the recently appointed editor of *The Throttle Flyer*, aspired to be the head of a tabloid journal but so far his dreams had come to nothing. He continued to practise his banner headlines where he could but some said his approach to captions overstepped the mark and was not in keeping with a sleepy village paper. For example, his headline reporting the simmering row between the church bell ringers and the immediate neighbours who brought out an injunction to have them stopped read: '*Gong bangers wrangle clanger*'

However, the one that won him the prize for bad taste was about a jumble sale that raised money for a sick girl's operation: '*Cash for trash pays for slash*'

When the news broke about the cricket club, it was no surprise to see on the hoarding outside the local newsagents: '*Cup boob club to go bust, sec' fails to keep abreast*'

This headline had the other employees at the paper wincing, but they went ahead with it anyway.

Arnold's main problem was the lack of news.

'Martin!' he shouted. 'What have we got today?'

Martin flicked over his journalist's spiral-bound pad. 'Er, one lost cat, a fire in the rubbish bin outside the chippy, had to evacuate the café. Big news that, eh?' he chuckled.

Arnold mused as he sucked the blunt end of his pencil, and then smiled. '*Roast cat menu shocks diners,*' he said as he wrote.

'You can't print that,' replied Martin.

'Why not?' asked Arnold, winking fitfully.

'Because it's not true,' Martin said, tilting his head.

'You can't prove it's not true, can you? Anyway, who says it has to be true?' Arnold reasoned. 'And if anyone has the balls to complain, we print an apology on the back page. Simple.'

'One day, one day it will all come crashing round your ears,' Martin predicted under his breath. Then he spun round on his chair. 'Are you going to the meeting?' he asked mischievously.

'Thinking about it... why?' Arnold hedged.

'He has been on from the club, says he's going to pull your frigging head off, unquote.'

'Best keep it down then,' Arnold whispered.

Throttle Village Hall:
7pm, the Show Begins

The village hall was full prior to the allotted time, partly due to concern about a village amenity, but mostly because there was nothing on TV and, rumour had it, there was more than a slight chance of a ding-dong.

John Appleby opened proceedings. 'Thanks for coming. Nice to see such a large audience, so without further ado … we'll get on with it.'

He was just about to when a voice he recognised echoed from deep down in the audience. 'Resign, resign, resign.'

Everyone turned to see a spotty youth going bright red with the attention.

'I won't resign just because you were dropped from the second team, Craig Williamson.'

Named, shamed and now humbled, Craig slumped in silence.

John continued. 'This is a serious matter, not helped by crap like this,' and he held aloft a copy of *The Throttle Flyer*. 'Tabloid journalism at its worst, and if the little shit who wrote it would stay behind, there's a few of us who would like a word.'

Up until then Arnold Bosworth had sat anonymously at the back taking notes. On hearing what was to him praise indeed, he wrote 'Yes' in large capitals as if he had won a prize, then he added the name Craig Williamson to his notes.

Unaware of Arnold Bosworth's presence, John continued. 'This is about the future of the club, a club that has been the mainstay of the village, where all classes of folk can play as equals.'

In the audience, eyeballs rolled back and stared at the ceiling as he slipped into Winston Churchill mode. Then he paused for a moment, took hold of the lapels of his jacket and took a deep breath. 'Where men are men and–'

'And women make the teas!' shouted a woman from the back of the hall.

John raised himself onto his toes, lifted his glasses and peered at where he thought the comment had come from. A ripple of laughter indicated he should abandon his speech.

'Over to you, Mr Padstow,' he sighed and passed over the microphone.

On receiving it, Arthur tapped the end and blew on it. 'Can you hear me?' he shouted.

The audience groaned with embarrassment.

'Bleedin' Laurel and Hardy … get on with it!' shouted an exasperated man at the front.

'Aye well, the options are limited,' he informed the now restless gathering. 'We either win something and the status quo remains, or we don't and it becomes a building site... and we don't want that, do we?'

The audience began to mumble with indecision.

'Be nice to have a new house. Don't like cricket anyway,' a woman said in a shrill voice, amusing the people sitting close to her.

Arthur put his hand over the microphone and turned to the others. 'Jesus,' he blurted out. However, his hand did not prevent the remark being heard around the room.

'He won't help you,' shouted a man at the back.

Also at the back of the audience, three men were quietly smiling at one another.

'Piece of cake, easy-peasy, the words "a piss-up" and "brewery" come to mind,' confirmed Joseph Lagg, the local estate agent, to the two Jakeson brothers at his side who were beginning to wonder why they were there.

John Appleby took hold of the microphone.

'Order, order, can we have some hush?' he said, spitting on the front row in the process. To ensure complete silence, he waved his arms as if flagging down a car.

'We have an announcement. In order to help us with our predicament, we have enlisted the help of a professional – but no ordinary professional. On your behalf we have called upon the very able Mr Benjamin Saxon, a big lad from Jamaica.'

Screwed-up faces in the audience suggested a lack of familiarity with the name.

'Well, not exactly from Jamaica, Leeds to be precise. Well, he lives in Leeds at the moment. To be honest, we don't know where he comes from,' he added, looking for support from the others, but none came.

'Anyway,' he shouted, regaining his thread, 'it'll cost and as the cricket club has nowt, we were hoping that you, the people that this club serves, will either dig in your pockets and donate a few quid, or come up with some fund-raising ideas.'

The deafening noise of mumbling and chairs being scraped back erupted. The moment he mentioned the word 'donation', people started to leave.

'Before you go, are there any questions?' he hastily added.

A giggly girl put her hand up.

'Yes love,' he asked patronisingly.

'How big... is big?' she said, unable to control her laughter.

'Six feet six and hands like shovels,' he replied, puzzled as the audience fell about.

'That *is* big,' she confirmed enthusiastically.

Arnold, still with his head down, scribbled furiously. 'New pro excites nympho: that's the back page done,' he mused. At the bottom of the page he scribbled, 'Bitter young man, could be useful' next to Craig Williamson's name.

Old Goat Brewery:
Geoffrey's New Career?

Geoffrey Perkins arrived at his new employer's premises. He gazed through the rusty wrought-iron gates at the somewhat dilapidated façade that revelled in times past: SUTCLIFFE'S PIES AND PUDDINGS ARE THE BEST. A more modest plastic sign bearing a goat's head indicated the building's present use.

'What the hell have I let myself in for?' he sighed, fighting back the desire to head off back down the M1. He entered the dimly lit office through a door marked MEAT DELIVERIES. His heart was sinking fast and he was just about to call it quits when a voice behind him blocked his escape.

'Welcome welcome' said Anthony Dawes, owner of the brewery. He put a too-familiar arm around Geoffrey's shoulder and went on, 'It might not look much but we like to call it home.'

He led Geoffrey towards a room that was white tiled from floor to ceiling, with no windows and no door. He pointed towards a plastic-topped table and a well-used office chair.

'Home... yes... home,' Geoffrey muttered.

'Now then, I've got a busy schedule this morning. We are testing a new batch, so you have a shufty round with Jonathan here, then we'll have a meet. Is that OK? About half ten in here?'

Geoffrey nodded then stood to shake hands with a young man who looked like he was employed more for his brawn than his brain.

'Meet, in here, coincidence that,' he replied, but the joke was lost.

Geoffrey wandered around the brewery savouring the smell of the hops and barley. He was not a brewer, neither did he understand the complexities of all the pipe work and vessels. He just liked the taste of beer.

Later, they sat at the table in Anthony Dawes's cluttered office.

'It's quite simple really; we have to sell more beer. The other bloke, the one who died, started a scheme where we sponsor all the local cricket clubs. Every player who scores a six or a four gets a free bottle of Owd Tup. Then we hope they like it so much they get it put on permanent behind the bar. So it's up to you to finalise it before the season starts.'

'Owd Tup, fine,' said Geoffrey, beginning to think he was on a different planet. 'Just one thing, what did the other bloke die of?'

'His liver packed in,' replied Anthony.

'Right,' sighed Geoffrey.

Geoffrey explained the strategy to Susan that evening.

'So let me get this straight!' she shrieked. 'You have to go round to that cricket club and suggest that every time they put our windows in, they get a free pint!'

Before he could explain, she ran upstairs and locked herself in the bedroom.

Lagg's Estate Agents:
Just Another Day?

Susan, who had not slept and still had not calmed down, entered the premises of Joseph Lagg Estate Agent.

'Can I help you, madam?' said the secretary in a voice which really meant, 'Can't you see I am in the middle of reading my magazine?'

'I need a word with Mr Lagg, if that's possible,' said Susan sharply.

'I'll see if he's available,' replied the secretary. She spun round on her chair and disappeared into the back office. 'Lady to see you, Mr Lagg.'

'Can you deal with it, Julia?' Lagg replied without looking up from his crossword. 'Four letter word for tug... pull?' he mused.

'Jerk,' she said in a low voice. He scowled at her. 'Look, she's asked to see you personally.'

'OK, OK, just give me five minutes.'

Julia returned to her desk and her magazine. 'He will be out in a minute, Mrs...'

'Perkins,' said Susan.

Moments later Susan was ushered into the back office. 'Untidy desk, untidy mind,' she thought.

'Mrs Perkins, how can I help you?'

'You can start by getting me and my family out of that house that you fraudulently sold us.'

There was a pause as he contemplated the term. 'Fraudulently, you say,' he repeated as a young couple entered the shop.

'Yes, fraudulently, F, R, A, U–' she dictated.

'Yes, yes, I know how to spell it, thanks,' said Joe, trying to keep his voice down.

'You sold us a house fraudulently by not informing us of the potential dangers of living there.' Susan added volume for effect. She turned to the couple who were standing near the open door listening. 'He did, you know. I wouldn't buy a house off him, he's a con man.'

The couple turned and left without shutting the door.

'And what's more, if you don't come up with something, I'll spread it all over town about what you've done. By the time I've finished, you'll not be able to sell a dog kennel, let alone a house.' Susan felt as though she had won the first round so she walked to the door.

'Mrs Perkins, come and sit down. Let's see if we can resolve the matter. Coffee?' Lagg said. He peered over her shoulder but the day's first potential customers had gone.

He showed Susan to a seat then paused and turned to his secretary. 'Two cups of coffee Julia, and wipe that smile off your face or it's back to the job club. Take a seat, Mrs Perkins.'

He had ushered Susan towards an inferior typist's chair compared to his own armchair-style seat. She immediately spotted the difference and set about him again.

'I can take you to court, you know, and get damages, reimbursement, compensation, restitution and reparation,' she said, making it up as she went along.

'Mrs Perkins, what's wrong with your house?' Lagg asked as Julia rattled in with the coffee.

'Our house is under siege during the cricket season. If one of us gets killed, it will be your fault because you failed to advise us of that fact.'

Julia tried hard not to smile, but Joe noticed the corners of her mouth twitch. 'That will be all, Julia.'

'You won't get me to admit it. It's that bloke you bought it off you should be suing,' he said, testing her out.

'He's abroad somewhere, but as the go-between you should have told us of any potential danger,' Susan responded, sensing she had the upper hand.

'Now look,' Lagg rounded. 'You got that house cheap, very cheap, plus all those carpets and fittings.' Then he paused. 'But if it's any consolation, you – we, that is – could sell it for a quick profit.' He considered he had said too much. 'I … I … can't say any more,' he stuttered. 'But you'll be grateful to me, just you see.'

'How?' she probed.

'I've told you, I can't say any more.'

'You'd better be bloody right or your name will be shit, do you hear,' she said, causing him to sit up again. 'Next time I call … you'd better have some answers.' She stared icily at him, stood up and walked out.

Lunchtime:

A Meeting of Sick Minds

The Old Goat Brewery Company had bought the local pub and then set about refurbishing it to make it look even older. They removed all the original fittings then replaced them with pseudo old pub furnishings. To some of the locals it was a perfect example of 'fixing something that weren't broke in the first place'.

In the back room, Joseph Lagg was relating the earlier episode with Susan to Roland Bullock. 'I'm telling you, this woman's trouble. She will ruin me if we don't do something,' he blubbered.

'Well, we are doing something,' Roland reassured softly, but then within a split second, turned. 'You didn't tell her anything, did you? If I find out that-'

'No, no, nothing,' stuttered Joe, clearly shaken by the threat.

'Don't give me that. You lie for a living, what have you said?' Roland hissed.

'Nothing, honest. Well, only that if she hangs on she will be able to sell her house at a profit.'

'Are you sure you didn't say any more?' probed Roland. 'Absolutely.'

'Look,' said Roland softly but with grit in his voice, 'all you have to do is make sure they have a shit season. Shouldn't be too difficult, they have one every year.'

They grinned, and then Joseph went serious again. 'But now they've got this new pro, this big coloured lad. Hell of a reputation, they're all on about him, 'specially the women. He were over at Dabbington last year.'

'Right,' interrupted Roland. 'Sounds like he puts it about, so you go over there and see if he caused any bother. Bound to have upset some bint. You know the old saying, "Hell hath no fury like a woman who's been two-timed".'

A sickly grin came over Joseph's face that indicated he did not have a clue what Roland was on about, but did not like to say.

Throttle Cricket Club Meeting:
Some Answers

After the usual chit-chat, the meeting got underway. Arthur Padstow read the secretary's report.

'I have to report, Mr Chairman, that we've had several offers of ways to raise money, some good, some not so good and one or two physically impossible... for me at least.'

He held aloft a scrap of paper. 'This one says it would be best to turn this place into a strip club. Says it's full of tits already, might as well be proper ones.'

A booming voice brought the dirty laughs to a halt. 'Mr Chairman, can this meeting be brought to order. I thought we were here to have a serious discussion.' Clearly upset by the smut, Janice rummaged in her handbag for a tissue.

'Can we have a bit of order here, gentlemen?' said John, wiping the tears of laughter from his eyes. 'Arthur, will you carry on?'

'Yes, well, er, another says we could set fire to the club and use the insurance money. Could be something in that. What do you think, nice holiday out of it as well?'

'Are you serious or what?' responded Tom.

Fred Pickup butted in when he felt that his reputation was at stake. 'Mr Chairman, can I just point out that if there are any more references to immorality, unlawful acts, fraud, etc. then you can have my resignation here and now.'

'Now see what you've done,' said Janice angrily, glaring at Arthur.

'There will be no more references to fraud or any wrongdoing, will there, Arthur?' added John.

'Err... no,' he said remorsefully.

'Karaoke nights are popular these days,' said John, hastily changing the subject. 'Charge an entrance fee, put a few pence on a pint and you've cracked it.'

'I like that idea,' said Janice, beginning to smile. 'It's a while since we had a sing-song. Be good for the community, we could put on a hotpot.'

'I don't think you understand what a karaoke is, do you Janice?' intervened Tom.

'Course I do. It's where we all get together and have a sing-song. I think it's a wonderful idea.' She smiled.

The others smiled back at her somewhat falsely, then Tom added with a grin, 'It'll give us chance to show off the new black pro. They can see what we need the money for. Mind you, we'll have to get some fresh beer in. They'll never buy this crap.'

As if to prove the distastefulness of the beer, he produced a belch that not only shook the rafters, but also disgusted all present.

'Mr Chairman,' interrupted Janice. 'I have to take exception to the terrible reference to "the new black pro". It's offensive and racist. Benjamin is a gentleman, which is more than can be said for some folk round here.'

'Point taken, you'll have to be more careful, Tom. We can't go round upsetting people, not right now.'

'Sorry Janice,' apologised Tom, putting on a pained expression as he patted his bulging stomach. 'Gas, terrible gas,' he added for effect.

There was a momentary pause as the committee pondered his words, and all were grateful when another member changed the subject.

'Can I have a word Mr Chairman?' interjected Fred Pickup, raising his hand formally.

'Carry on.'

'Thank you, Mr Chairman. I have to point out to the committee that a karaoke night is not going to pay for all Benjamin's expenses. We still need a minimum of six grand just for his wages.'

The phrase 'six grand' was repeated around the table, each time with added emphasis.

'So we've still a lot of work to do. Mind you, now that he is lodging with Janice, we don't have to cough up for his digs.'

The rest of the committee stared cynically in Janice's direction.

'Gentleman, is he?' said Tom, avoiding her gaze by inspecting the murk in his glass.

Tom Deakin Cold Calls the Brewery

'Hello there, my name's Tom. I'm from the cricket club up the road, and I was wondering if you could help us out?'

Anthony Dawes could not believe his ears. 'Come on in, come on in... fancy a pint?'

Tom could not believe his ears either. 'A bit early, but go on,' he replied, as though they were twisting his arm.

Moments later, he held aloft a foaming glass straight from the barrel. He was so surprised with his good fortune that he had to blink to make sure he was not dreaming.

'We call it Old Goat's Horn. What do you think?' grinned Anthony.

'Soddin' hell, that is strong,' he replied, exhaling as if he had consumed something peppery.

'Only supposed to have it in halves by rights. Seven point five per cent alcohol. It comes under the heading of extra strong ale,' Anthony advised.

'Is that seven point five on the Richter scale?' Tom said, draining the glass.

'We have weaker ale, a three point nine, for the ordinary punters … like to try it?' offered Anthony.

'Never been known to refuse. What's this called, Ram's Bollocks?' he replied jovially.

'It's Old Tup... play on words. Head-banging stuff, took us ages to come up with that,' Anthony boasted proudly.

Tom finished his pint. 'This'll do fine. Don't want them getting pissed too quickly or they'll not be able to buy no more,' he cackled. 'Could I test one more Old Goat's Horn, just to make absolutely sure?'

'Aye but be careful, it'll creep up on you,' warned Anthony.

Ten minutes later, Anthony arrived back with Geoffrey to see Tom mellowing nicely.

'I'd like you to meet Geoffrey Perkins, our sales managing director.'

Geoffrey raised his eyebrows when he heard his new title then held out his hand. 'Pleased to meet you.'

Tom looked in his direction but could not focus any more. 'Too strong for t'punters,' he confirmed, slurring his words.

'Give us a hand to take him round back till he sobers up. Can't have him being ill in here.'

Karaoke Night: A Good Do?

The clubhouse was scheduled for a coat of paint for the 'Karaoke and Meet the Pro Night', as it was billed. However, the committee decided on low-wattage lighting instead.

The attraction of the 'large coloured gentleman' had ensured a good turnout, which unfortunately threw up other issues.

'Beer's going down a treat,' grinned Tom, feeling vindicated about the choice. 'But whatever you do, don't put the barrel on that's in the back. It's a little stronger and for a very special occasion,' he instructed David, one of the players who was helping behind the bar.

Eager to make Benjamin feel at home, Tom approached him with a foaming pint. 'Here, get this down your neck. Careful though, a few of these and you won't know what day it is.'

Tom watched in amazement as Ben's huge hand wrapped around the glass and he literally poured the beer down in one go. 'Deeeeelicious, does it have a name?' he posed.

'Well er, aye, Old Tup. Couple of these and you'll tup anything.'

'Then we'll have to put it to the test' Ben said, letting his accent drag the maximum from each vowel. His group of admirers, eager to please, fell about in affected laughter.

'I've heard you don't mess about,' chirped one of them.

'Right,' he drawled. 'Youse gotta be as slow as a stopped clock and as hot as mustard.'

There was a pause as they worked it out. A woman who was earwigging grabbed the bar rail for support as her legs gave way.

David the helper was enjoying life behind the bar until the bitter pump began to emit only froth. 'Tom, help, beer's running out,' he shouted over the heads of the mass of people holding empty pint pots in the air.

'Funny feeling this would happen,' Tom mused as he made his way toward the cluttered little room behind the bar amusingly called 'the cellar'.

John Appleby, who was doing a spot of circulating at the time, spotted the concern on his face. 'You alright?' he asked.

'Na. Beer's going down faster than I thought, only one barrel left.'

'So what's the problem? Get it on then.'

'The one that's left is a bit stronger, that's all. I was saving it…' he broke off to choose the right words. 'For a special occasion,' he went on.

'Aye, like cutting the grass. We're not bleeding daft, you know,' John said knowingly.

'It'll have to go on. This lot will go mad if we run out,' Tom added with concern.

'OK, but we'll have to warn them, this stuff is lethal.'

He fought his way to the front of the room then addressed the assembled guests from a makeshift stage. He grabbed the microphone, tapped it then began to speak.

'Ladies and gentlemen, can I have your attention please? I would just like to thank you for your attendance tonight and for making this a great do. I hope you have all had a chance to meet Benjamin and to find out what a nice chap he is. I know he's already got his eye on one or two of you young ladies.'

The committee and most of the audience cringed.

'He hasn't a clue,' Tom whispered to Arthur Padstow.

John, unaware of their anxiety, plodded on with his speech. 'I would also like to take the opportunity of advising you that the ordinary beer has run out, and we have to put on the emergency barrel. Old Goat's Horn is its name, for some reason. Problem is it's twice as strong so we're only serving it in halves... and I'm afraid it's twice the price.'

Then as a hasty afterthought, 'Oh, and before I forget, could you put your hands together for the ladies who organised the pie and peas. Thank you.'

John's plea for recognition of the women's efforts went unheard as the majority of the audience rushed towards the bar, whilst at the same time complaining about the cost.

Not long afterwards, heads began to spin and legs began to wobble. Those who decided they had had enough attempted to leave, but as soon as the fresh air hit them they found that they couldn't remember the way home. Many squatted on the pitch, pointing at the moon for guidance before slowly sinking into the foetal position. Oblivious to the chill of the night and the continuous din from the karaoke, deep sleep was now the only act they could achieve.

The Results of a Good Night's Work

Early next morning, Arthur and Tom surveyed the damage at the cricket club.

'Don't tell me I didn't frigging warn you. It's like a plane crash, bodies everywhere, all over the field, up the frigging sight screen. Some idiot tried to get the bleeding roller going. I tell you, we'd have had fatalities if they'd succeeded.'

He glanced across the pitch to where a small white car with a blue light pulled up on the road. 'That's all we need, PC Plod.'

The local constable eased his large frame out of the driver's door then put on his helmet; he slammed the door then strode slowly but purposefully towards them. He adopted the approach of a man whose peaceful Sunday morning had been disrupted way too early.

'Judging by his face, he's a bit hacked off,' whispered Tom.

The policeman stood next to them and silently surveyed the scene, then turned back and stared at them.

'We've had complaints about the racket from three miles away. One bloke said he heard "My, My, Delilah" six times. Said he used to be a fan of Tom Jones but not any more. You've upset the whole neighbourhood. What's going on?'

'Bit of a welcome party, meet the pro,' said Arthur.

'Goat's Horn,' added Tom. 'I told 'em not to.'

'Don't take the piss,' said the PC, leaning so far forward that their noses touched.

'No, Goat's Horn, it's a beer, only it were a bit too powerful for the locals. I'm afraid some of them got carried away.'

'Some of them! Some of them!' repeated the PC. Then he went on, 'All of them, I'd say. This is a peaceful village, quiet, know what I mean? So don't you go wrecking it with your soddin' sheep dip.'

'Goat's Horn,' Tom corrected him politely.

'Whatever. Be warned, it comes under the heading of running an unruly house, causing a disturbance, an affray, not to mention drinking after hours. They could throw the book at you, all of you, all the committee. Put you behind bars, sewing bags, eating porridge, sleeping with queers for the rest of your natural. Be warned.' The PC turned and walked to his car, smirking.

'Porridge is alright, not keen on the rest,' laughed Tom.

Halfway across the pitch, the involuntary heaving noise emitted by another ashen figure throwing up against the clubhouse wall made the constable pause, but only momentarily.

Just Another Day in
the Bullock Household?

The breakfast table had been cleared away and Sir Alf was getting himself psyched up for his new pastime, aptly named 'find the lady'. This was a game conducted within the confines of the house and with the primary objective of giving him a purpose and easing his boredom.

Still not having come to terms with his semi-confinement after a lifetime of constant activity, he had decided that the parts of his body that were still functioning should remain so; if you don't use it, you are more than likely to lose it. Consequently he had invented this work-out for his arms and mind. The rules were similar to hide and seek: Flora had five minutes or so to hide then Sir Alf had to find her within a certain time, usually half an hour.

Unbeknown to Lady Miriam, this pastime was the primary cause of the damage to the interior of the house as Sir Alf raced from room to room with the clock ticking.

It was rare for Sir Alf to find Flora within the allotted time but on the occasions that he did, they both ended up laughing aloud. As they grew to know each other better, they found they could talk quite openly. As the weeks went by they became quite close, a fact that confused Alf no end.

'All new ground to me,' he pondered after Flora had gone home. Then one day after he had failed yet again to find her, she really put the wind up him.

'You know, we can spice this game up a bit if you like,' she said quietly, with more than a hint of embarrassment.

He cleared his throat. 'What do you mean, spice it up?'

Flora started to blush. 'Well, I'm a bit short of cash, and you must be a bit … you know.'

'A bit what?' he questioned.

'You know, short of the other.'

'And how have you come to that deduction, young lady?' said Sir Alf, a bit put out.

'Well it's obvious, the way you two carry on. Can't be much love between you.'

He stiffened in his chair. 'You are putting more than two and two together and assuming the worst.' Then he pondered. 'I have to admit, love and affection seem a thing of the past these days,' he sighed. Then the frustration got the better of him. 'It's only my legs that are useless, you know. The rest of me is OK.'

'Hey, you don't have to convince me, I'm the one who picks up the forks every morning.'

Sir Alf looked down. 'What a bugger... but how did you?'

'No problem.'

'So what were you thinking?'

There was a pause whilst Flora summoned the courage to speak. 'Well... I go and hide, as usual, and if you find me within the time then, well... you know.' She stopped and turned away.

'And if I don't find you, what then?' he asked.

'You give me ten quid,' she added quickly.

'Ten quid, you must be joking!' he shouted. Flora looked shocked. 'Nothing less than twenty-five.' He grinned.

Her shocked expression gave way to a wry smile. 'Till tomorrow then,' she said and she winked at him.

He winked back awkwardly. As she walked down the drive, he watched her from the doorway. 'Haven't felt like this in years,' he told the empty house as he turned and shut the door. 'Feel like a kid on a first date.'

He clicked on the kettle in the kitchen and pondered the past hour. The possible consequences kept going round in his head. He stared at the kettle as the steam began to pour from the spout.

'I'll be in hot water if this gets out. What the hell have I gone and done?' he asked the teapot. Then, as he dunked his digestive, he looked up at the walls and ceiling. 'What's to lose?' he mused. 'Sod all,' he concluded as the end fell off his biscuit.

Yet Another Cricket Club Meeting

Janice, stony faced, stood outside the door waiting to be let in. She purposefully looked the other way as Arthur approached, pointing the key towards the lock. As he opened the door, a waft of disinfectant fumes hit him.

'Bleeding hell, what's that?' he remarked as his eyes started to run.

'It's the result of all my cleaning,' barked Janice.

They left the door open and opened the one window that worked.

'Now then, will anyone second the minutes of the previous meeting?' The chairman looked round.

'This is a farce! There's only four of us, we'll be here all night,' said Tom, gesturing impatience by folding his arms.

'You have to observe the rules of running a meeting,' said Arthur haughtily.

'I know, rules is rules. Just get on with it,' said Tom, reluctantly raising his hand.

John nodded towards Janice who was taking down the minutes. 'Seconded by Tom Deakin.' He cleared his throat, more for effect than need. 'I think we can all say that the "Meet the Pro Night" was a success. Certainly everyone I've spoken to enjoyed themselves.'

Janice raised her hand. 'Mr Chairman!' she shouted. 'So the concept of somebody enjoying themselves is based on whether they are paralytic or not, is it? Well, I think it is a disgrace. There were people being ill all over the place. And you,' she pointed at Tom, 'obviously didn't get involved in the clean-up. It was disgusting, sick everywhere, the place stank to high heaven. You can still smell it now. We had to use over a gallon of bleach.'

'And now it stinks like a public lav,' he observed dryly.

'OK, let's get back to business,' John intervened. He turned and beckoned at the treasurer. 'It was also a fund-raising night. How did we do, Fred?'

Fred, a studiously plain speaker whose clean-cut appearance reflected the way he did the finances, said, 'Well, Mr Chairman, I've worked it all out and taking into account the cost of cleaning sundries purchased the following day, the event made two hundred and fifteen pounds.'

'Not bad, eh,' said Arthur positively.

Fred interjected in his official, dour manner, and they instinctively knew it would be bad news. 'Mr Chairman, can I put this into perspective? We said we would pay Benjamin six grand, that is, three hundred a week. We have paid him one week's pay. We owe him two, and we have fifty-six pounds in the bank.'

One by one, mouths fell open as the dire circumstances registered.

'On a happy note, beer's OK,' said Tom, consuming it with his usual relish.

'Mr Chairman. The logic of the situation is that we need a "Meet the Pro" night each week, just to break even,' he advised, more in jest than fact.

Everyone apart from Janice looked up and smiled. Instead, she issued a warning. 'If you think I'm cleaning up the mess every Sunday, you must be bloody mad – and that's swearing.'

The meeting over, Tom and Arthur were in discussion, leaning against the bar sampling the latest offering from the brewery.

'We need a do that won't cause a lot of noise, doesn't need a crowd and that a select few would be willing to pay good money for.'

In unison they whispered, 'A strip night,' followed by a dirty laugh.

Joe Lagg:

Start of a Bad Day

The sun was streaming through the window of J. Lagg, Estate Agents. Joe was in a good mood as he stuck bogus sold stickers onto details of bogus houses.

'Got to get the housing market moving somehow, create a bit of panic. A legitimate tactic,' he told himself.

Julia, his secretary, was giving him a piece of her mind after he had moved her desk next to the shop window. 'I'm quite fond of the sun myself, Tenerife, Ibiza or Malaga, anywhere really, but not when it's glaring onto the computer screen. If there are any errors, it's not down to me. Daft idea, everyone who walks past gawps at me, gives me the creeps.'

'We've got to give the high-tech impression. It's what the punter wants, see their name on a print-out, they go for it,' he reassured in a false 'Jack-the-lad' accent.

'Still a crap idea,' she pressed.

The futility of the argument got the better of him so he retired to the back office and the quick crossword. A couple of easy clues focused his attention, so he did not hear the door open as Julia poked her head through. Seeing he was miles away, she raised her voice above the normal volume required for communicating with someone not more than six feet away.

'Sorry to disturb your important meeting but there's a Mrs Perkins to see you,' she yelled.

The freshly made coffee he held in his hand spilled as he jumped and the newspaper accurately funnelled the drink neatly into his lap. 'No, no!' he shouted as the hot liquid seeped through to his underwear.

'Mission accomplished,' thought Julia.

'You can go through now,' she advised Susan cheerily.

Susan's expression was puzzled. 'Are you sure he's ready?' she queried.

'Oh yes,' Julia replied. 'He's a high-tech professional,' she added as she went back to her seat in the window.

Susan entered the office to see Joseph standing with his legs apart and pulling at the front of his fly. Taking advantage of his dilemma, she did not hesitate.

'Always wet yourself when you hear my name, do you? Well, you'll do much worse if things don't begin to move.'

He ushered her to a seat whilst continuing to hold out the front of his trousers. 'Mrs Perkins, please sit down. Let's discuss this, peaceable like.'

'So, what have you done then?' she asked, trying to maintain her aggression.

Sitting back in his chair and still dabbing his trousers with a tissue, he explained. 'Well, er, nothing. You see, we have to be patient, we are playing a waiting game.'

Susan leapt in again. 'So how long are we going to be patient for? A week, a fortnight?'

Joseph looked at the cardboard, pyramid-shaped calendar on his desk. 'Well, by my calculations, another seventeen weeks.'

'Curious amount of time?' she queried.

Julia, who had been hesitating at the door with a tray of coffee, offered, as Joseph put it later, an unhelpful input. 'Longer, if we get through the next round,' she said cryptically and left.

Still puzzled, Susan asked, 'What does she mean?'

'Nothing, just ignore her. Got it on her today. Look, if all goes according to plan, it will be just seventeen weeks.'

They finished the coffee in silence. Joseph looked through the window. It had clouded over and had started to rain.

'At least she'll be able to see the bloody screen,' he muttered.

Later the Same Day:
The Perkins' House

Geoffrey was analysing the deadlines and target figures issued by his new boss. 'I'll never achieve these, not in the time that's left,' he said desperately.

Hearing his plight from the kitchen and working on the premise that a trouble shared is a trouble doubled, Susan offered only a modicum of support. 'Achieve what, in what time?'

Geoffrey, panicking, tried to explain. 'He wants me to sell three barrels of each beer to each cricket club in the Nethersdale League by the end of the season.'

'That must be ages off. You can do that,' she said supportively, not knowing if he could or not.

Geoffrey continued, his voice sounding more strained. 'Seventeen weeks is all that's left, and most have already got fixed up with ale!' Beads of sweat formed on his brow. He waited for a reply that would at least go some way to solve the problem.

Susan, though, had switched off the moment he mentioned the timescale. 'Coincidence, never,' she whispered. She put her head round the door. 'What's seventeen weeks?'

'You're not listening!' shouted Geoffrey as the frustration got the better of him. 'It's all that's left of the cricket season, except for them that gets through to the next round.'

Susan went back to the ironing. 'What are you up to Mr Lagg?'

Roland Bullock:
The Story so Far

As boss of Bullock Units Limited, Roland allowed himself a few luxuries. A new Jaguar, membership of the local but prestigious Premier Golf Club, and even what was laughingly called a 'private box' at Hallifield Football Club.

'For entertaining friends and business colleagues,' he told the groundsman, who, for the purposes of conducting the transaction, had acquired the title of Director of Corporate Accommodation.

As he signed the cheque for another season, the chap replied in a completely unimpressed manner. 'Whatever you want, lad.'

Roland looked round at the cold, stark, whitewashed walls that bore the names of sponsors. 'It's always cold here,' he said, then added, 'Concrete, bricks, whitewash, and it stinks of liniment and piss.'

'You don't have to come here,' replied the man, replacing his tweed jacket with a brown smock.

'You're right, I don't.' Roland had few friends and even fewer business colleagues, so the box remained empty most of the time. These extravagances, or 'rightful perks of the job' as he put it, devoured his money. 'It's OK, because it's the company's money, tax deductible,' he tried to convince himself when the invoices needed signing. The fact was, though, he could not play golf very well and he was not that interested in football. He would show some excitement when he sank a putt or the home team scored, but most of the time he switched off and wondered what they saw in it, and why he was there in the first place.

Cruising round in his new car was all right but he did not go anywhere other than to work and back. The car was so smooth and quiet that he felt he was in a steel box, cut off from other people, their lives, their interests, their fun, so the novelty of that soon wore off too. He was lonely and he knew it.

Sometimes he would sit behind the wheel at traffic lights and shout, 'I am so pissed off! Is this what it's all about? Just what the hell am I doing with my life?' If his tormented speech was a cry for help, it failed, because sound will not transmit through a soundproofed car.

He had acquaintances; he called them friends but they were only around during the football season or up for a free game of golf at his club. Other than these people, he couldn't think of a single person he could relate to or confide in. 'Is it me or them or what?' he would contemplate when feeling low.

He hated his childhood; it was his dad's fault, even though he rarely saw him, because he was too busy running his smelly mill. 'His dirty, horrible, stinking mill.'

'All this will be yours one day,' his dad promised, but he did not want it then and he wanted it even less now.

He christened it, 'The millstone around my frigging neck'.

The other blight on his upbringing was his education. Worried about Roland's 'lack of nous', his dad sent him to public school in order to 'wake him up a bit'.

Roland hated that too. For some reason he did not get on with the other boys and it upset him terribly. 'Why is it always me the jokes are played on?' he wondered.

He tried to lose his broad accent in an effort to fit in. It appeared to work for a while but after one tutor, a Mr Smythe, who had a pronounced speech impediment, referred to him as 'Master Bollock', the ribbing started again.

The other boys thought it hilarious to sketch a single hairy testicle across his work. He lay in his dormitory quietly sobbing with thoughts of escape running through his mind, but where to? He hated school and he hated home.

Roland did not have much luck with the cricket either. His dad, who effectively owned the club, pulled a few strings to get him a place in the side, but after only three games he gave up. Unfortunately, when the word got out how he achieved selection, his credibility sank to an all-time low. From then on he stayed away from the club and his deep-seated desire for revenge increased and intensified. Revenge became a word he used frequently when his mind drifted.

'My time will come,' he muttered when he recalled the treatment meted out to him by the players. Now and then, he dreamt about methods of retribution. It did not take much, just a pause in the traffic, and his thoughts would whizz around until the blaring horn of a vehicle brought him back to the present day.

'OK, OK, you bastard!' he shouted as he pulled away from the lights that had been green for what the lorry driver thought was a lifetime. 'But this isn't a day for being hacked off,' he reminded himself as he screeched into the courtyard of Bullock Units Limited. 'We've got ass to kick.'

After the collapse of the cotton trade, plain Alfred Bullock as he was then, snapped up the mill for a song and immediately sold all the cotton machinery to other countries which made garments and exported them back to this country at a profit. Some embittered members of the community suggested that it was these 'dealings', or more likely the greasing of palms, that earned him the knighthood. He also, without any compassion, sold the gleaming original steam engine for scrap. It was a tragic day for the workers when they witnessed the destruction of their livelihood.

Insult was added to injury twelve months later when he demolished all but the ground and first floors. 'Be easier to manage,' he reasoned.

There was no room for sentiment in the 'Alfred Bullock plan'. The parts that were useful and in one piece were sold, the rest broken up and sold as scrap. This applied to the mill engine, masonry, well-oiled hardwood floorboards, everything, until just two floors remained. These were divided into self-contained workshops and rented out to tenants on a yearly basis.

Roland enjoyed his position as proprietor. He breezed into the office that had not been redecorated since his father left. 'Crap,' he commented every time he passed the false oak panelled walls that wobbled if pressed. 'Christ knows why it's called beauty board,' he asked himself for the hundredth time.

He sat in the big PVC swivel chair that made rude noises every time he moved, then leaned forward and rested his arms on the grand, well-used desk rescued from the mill manager's office. It was among only a few items to survive the ransacking when Sir Alf acquired the mill.

Many a time Roland questioned his father's taste for mixing classic grandeur with modern trash. The so-called executive toys that were strategically placed for effect on the mahogany-topped desk highlighted this. He had thought about junking the lot, but on miserable days the chair was a source of amusement. He laughed like a drain during discussions with a prospective tenant, when the noise erupted at a crucial moment. He collapsed into a fit of laughter until the tears rolled down his face. Roland's dilemma was that the chair would look ridiculous in the presence of modern office furniture, so rather than lose his object of fun, he persevered with it.

He sat in the chair and announced in a booming voice to the walls, 'But today we have some rental contracts to re-negotiate. No time for sentimentality, serious business to attend to. Marion, bring in the renewals file.'

Marion, his long-suffering, middle-aged secretary, raised her eyes to the ceiling. She only worked mornings just to get out of the house. She could easily walk away but the job paid for the niceties in life and all she really had to do was put up with Roland.

'What happened to "please" and "thank you", you ignorant little shite?' she complained in a voice just low enough not to be heard.

One Such Tenant

Thomas Reagan, an electrical engineer who rented a unit from Roland, was about to have his day turned upside down.

'Yes, hello, what can I do you for?' He spoke into the telephone that was also a fax, a copier, a cassette player, a radio and an answerphone. He liked to portray an image of modernity, of only using the latest equipment but, as he had recently experienced, high-tech gadgetry can have a downside. When one of the resident rat population chewed through the mains cable, it not only sentenced Thomas to a day of zero communication with the outside world but also to total silence in his workshop. As he described it later to his wife, 'It was like being in solitary bloody confinement, with only the stench of burnt rat for company.'

'Can I help you?' he bellowed down the phone.

On the other end of the line Sir Alf, thinking the man must be deaf, replied at the same volume. 'Well I hope so, that's why I've rung!'

Sir Alf, not realising he was actually speaking to someone who rented a unit from him, paused. Thomas paused as well, and then shook the phone. 'Hello, you still there?'

'Jesus!' cried Sir Alf as he held the phone away to prevent his eardrums bursting. He carefully put the receiver back to his ear, and then decided to get in quick. 'I want this chair upgrading. It's too slow, can't catch her, costing a fortune,' he said rapidly. Then as he registered that he had gone too far, he backtracked. 'I just need it upgrading.'

'You've got the wrong number, it's a joiner you need.'

'No, no, an electrician,' he replied, realising the confusion he was causing. 'It's a wheelchair, an electric wheelchair, I want it upgrading. You know, faster, quicker and slicker and I want it to go over rough ground and for longer on a full charge,' he explained.

'Hang on, hang on, and let me get this straight. You want me to make an electric wheelchair do all that?'

'Are you, or are you not, an electrical engineer?' Alf said impatiently.

'Well, er, yes, it's just that it's a strange request, that's all,' Thomas added quickly, not wanting to throw business away. 'Never had this type of request before. It's usually vacs and washers. Best if I come and see the problem,' he suggested.

'If you're an electrical engineer, there is no problem,' responded Sir Alf.

'Still, it's best if I see the, er, chair. What's the address?'

Sir Alf spelt out the address and gave him directions.

'Fine Mr Bullock, big house, top of the hill, no problem. When are you in then?' he asked innocently.

'I'm here all the bloody time! That's what it's all about,' said Sir Alf, snapping and then wishing he had not.

'I'll just tidy up, then I'll set off.'

The pleasantries over, they both hung up.

'Bullock, big house, top of hill, that rings a small bell,' Thomas mused. He locked up the workshop and was just about to set off when Roland approached carrying a buff-coloured envelope. He had a swagger in his step and a smirk on his face.

'Ah, Mr Reagan, glad I caught you. How's business?' he asked.

'Fine, what do you want?' he answered abruptly.

'It's now twelve months since you started here. Hope everything's OK, but more to the point, it's time we discussed the rental arrangement for the next period.'

Thomas took the envelope and opened it. 'Some discussion, you robbing bastard!' he remarked on seeing the contents.

'Now, now, Mr Reagan, let's keep things civil.'

'It's gone up twenty per cent. Are you trying to ruin me?'

'You just said business was fine. And if you recall, the first twelve months is always at a reduced rate to allow you to settle in,' Roland explained in a falsely caring way.

Thomas glared at him. 'I seem to remember the word negotiation being used last year. This is bloody exploitation. You let me invest in a workshop, set it all up then dump this on me? Well you can stuff your contract up your arse. Call again when you want to discuss terms properly!' He threw the envelope and its contents on the floor.

As he drove to Sir Alf's house, Thomas's mind was full of devious plots of how to murder and then dispose of Roland Bullock. 'Murder's easy, but how do you buy twenty gallons of hydrochloric acid and not get noticed?' He pondered this dilemma as he knocked on the front door.

'Mr Reagan,' said Sir Alf, responding to the heavy-duty knock.

Thomas nodded.

Sir Alf observed the silence and sour expression. 'You OK?'

'Sorry, it's that bastard at Bullock Units, excuse the French,' Thomas said, warming to Sir Alf's concern. 'He's just gone and put...' His complaint tailed off as the penny dropped. 'Sorry, Mr Bullock, only just realised, it used to be your place,' he added, reddening with embarrassment.

'Still is my place. No need to be sorry, you're probably right. He is turning out to be a bit of a bugger.' Sir Alf looked at the floor. Now it was his turn to be embarrassed. 'Not a nice thing to say about your only son, but call a spade a spade.'

He paused as they made their way into the kitchen, then he looked up and smiled at Thomas as a scheme developed in his head. 'But we might be in a position to do each other a bit of good.'

Thomas looked at him sideways. 'Oh?' he said cautiously.

'How about if I sort out your rent and you sort out my chair … deal?'

Sir Alf waited as Thomas thought over the proposal. 'Deal,' he replied, holding his hand across the kitchen table and smiling for the first time that day.

The Bullock's Kitchen:
Suspicions Raised

As a token protest about the regular breakfast slanging match, Miriam had taken to having her breakfast in the kitchen perched on a stool. While Flora was watching the toast, Miriam was eyeing her up.

Flora had been making good use of her new income to pay off her visa, buy smart designer clothes and get a hairdo.

'Bit posh for doing housework in, aren't they?' said Miriam sarcastically.

Flora turned. 'I don't know what you mean.'

'You know what I mean. Your outfit, bit posh isn't it?'

'If you say so, Mrs Bullock,' said Flora, urging the toast to brown in order to escape the inquisition.

'It was you I saw shopping in AEROS the other day?' probed Miriam.

'Might have been, but I was only looking. Too expensive for me,' added Flora, giving nothing away.

'You look like you're after something, or someone,'

'Nothing to do with you, what I do,' Flora hissed, then sniffed the air and strutted into the breakfast room with the rack of toast.

Miriam followed, and Flora retreated to the kitchen. 'She's on the make; she's after our Roland.'

Roland and Sir Alf looked up from their papers and then, in disbelief, looked back down again. But when Flora came back in again with the coffee, Roland took more notice. He looked her up and down then, as their eyes met, he smiled and winked. Flora in reply put out her tongue.

'I don't think so, Mum,' he said.

'Well who else could it be?'

Sir Alf kept his head in his paper and pretended not to notice. Recently in the pursuance of her job as house cleaner, and as the hidden participant in the game of hide and seek, Flora had discovered many unused rooms in the Bullock house. This mercenary quest was to avoid using the same hiding place twice and thus keep the resulting cash flowing in. However, deep down inside she believed that she was being a bit hard, so when she discovered a neat little bedroom that looked as though it had not seen daylight for years, she realised how she could repay Sir Alf for all his generosity.

A Sunny Saturday Afternoon

Susan peered through the living-room window. She glowered at the mesh fence that had become the iron bars to her prison. 'You mustn't play in the front garden,' she said, wagging a finger at Alison. 'It's very dangerous. Those silly men out there could easily kill us if we set foot outside our own door.'

Susan was aware that her voice sounded a little cracked and paranoid. She clasped her hands to the sides of her head and looked down at her daughter.

'Can we play at the back?' Alison asked calmly.

'Er, yes, of course, good idea,' stuttered Susan, trying to regain her composure.

They held hands and were gingerly walking towards the garden when they heard a banging noise followed by a huge cheer. It was the sound of a ball hitting the mesh window guard and the subsequent applause was for a six hit by Benjamin.

He acknowledged the crowd's appreciation. However, as had been explained to him at the start of the season, there was a downside to lofting balls straight down the pitch. It was an unwritten club rule that if you knocked the ball into the gardens opposite, it was up to you to go and get it.

Meanwhile Susan and Alison, who were in the kitchen, were frozen to the spot.

'You stay there,' Susan whispered loudly, pointing underneath the kitchen table. Then she crept on all fours into the lounge.

'No damage so far,' she reassured Alison, pretending she was still in control.

She peered out of the window and she still could not see any signs of a disturbance. Becoming braver, she crept into the vestibule and opened the front door. What happened next was too much for her.

At the same time as she opened the door, Benjamin was about to press the doorbell. The sight of a huge hand coming straight for her astounded her.

Moments later, Benjamin was trying to explain to Susan the reasons for having to retrieve the ball, but with little success. 'You see, we gets awful grief from next door, so no one wants to fetch it.'

'How did I get here?' she asked, suddenly realising she was lying on her own settee.

'No problem, I just picked you up. Seemed the thing to do.'

'Yes, yes, of course,' she said, looking up at the man who had to bend his head to avoid touching the light fitting.

Susan thought she could deal with most situations, but she was shocked to find she could not take her eyes off the very prominent bulge in the front of his trousers. She had to fight back the intense urge to touch it.

'Are you all right, cos I gotta go? I'll call back later to make sure you're OK.'

Susan turned to see faces at the window. The other fielders had arrived to see what was causing the delay.

'Oh!' she yelped. She was confused, hot, and shaking. As he crossed the threshold of the front door, she was surprised to hear herself calling: 'Benjamin, when did you say you were coming?'

As they trotted across the field, the other players mimicked her. 'When are you coming? When are you coming?' they laughed aloud.

Benjamin grinned. 'Never fails. Soon as they see my huge box, they're hooked.'

Susan stared at the ceiling, which appeared to be spinning.

'Be out in a minute!' she called to Alison who was now playing in the garden. Susan felt strange; she was exhausted, tingling all over and although it was not particularly hot, she was sweating.

Later in the day, she confided this to one of the women she was friendly with on the school run. She stared into her coffee for inspiration, trying to make sense of it all. 'It was just as though I'd had, you know, dealings with him,' she explained cryptically, then coloured up with embarrassment.

'Well if that happens just by looking, imagine what the real thing could do for you,' said her friend, finishing the comment with a dirty laugh.

However, Susan was way ahead of her.

A Strip Night Is Suggested

'It's not a strip night. It's a men-only night with an exotic dancer,' Tom Deakin said unconvincingly. He was struggling to convince Arthur Padstow and John Appleby that this would be a good idea for raising funds.

'Janice will kill us if she finds out. How do we explain where the money comes from? Fred will not believe it's an anonymous donation. I tell you, it's fraught with problems.'

'Fred's in on it,' smiled Tom smugly.

'You're joking! That prude!'

'He might be a prude but he likes a gamble. He said it's ages since he had a game of brag and I've told him about the disco dancer.'

'Disco dancer, oh my God, this is getting worse,' said Arthur rubbing the perspiration from his forehead. 'He will go frigging mad when he finds out.'

'Well, he won't find out, will he, leastways not until it's too late, then we'll say they sent the wrong woman. Look, we have to have him in on this to shuffle the money so Janice will be none the wiser.'

'Let me get this straight,' said Arthur. 'You've told Fred that on the night we're having a game of dominoes, there's this woman coming round to dance for us. Jesus, he will hit the roof when he finds out.'

'I can't believe he's fallen for it,' said John shaking his head. Then, with a dirty leer, he probed, 'Where did you get this woman from, anyway?'

'Mate of mine put me on to this agency. She's only fifty quid.'

'You get what you pay for, you know. Must be a scrubber.'

The beer had loosened their inhibitions and, with tears of laughter rolling down his face, Tom added the final insult: 'Well if she's not up to it, she can help Janice clean out the club.'

Hide and Seek

Sir Alf had just had his best chase yet. He managed to get close to Flora's location, but his time ran out and those few seconds had cost him the statutory twenty-five pounds. 'Got to sort this out,' he thought as he handed over the cash whilst forcing a smile.

'Flora, I don't know where you hide these days. I'm losing track of the places to look.'

It was true, Flora found rooms covered in dust that had probably never been entered for years.

'If you think I'm giving my secrets away…' she laughed.

She reflected on the quandary of having a lucrative source of income but at the same time feeling rotten about not giving anything in return.

She kissed him on the forehead, then immediately wiped the lipstick away with the rag she used on the banister rail. 'Got to crack on,' she said cheekily. She wandered up the stairs, giving the rail an extra rub as she went.

'Got to get the odds more even,' Alf thought. He sneaked a look at Flora's legs as she skipped up the stairs. He sighed. Then, as she got out of earshot, he muttered, 'Not only is it costing me a mint, but it's rousing sensations I thought were long dead … must ring the man about the chair.'

He was hunting for the phone number when the doorbell rang. 'I'll get it!' he bellowed. He was wheeling himself to the door when it rang again. 'OK, OK!' he shouted impatiently, not knowing who was on the other side.

He opened the door to find John Appleby standing there. They looked at one another for what seemed ages.

Then Sir Alf broke the deadlock. 'Good Jesus, John, it's been a long time. Come in, come in.' John followed, but did not get a word in. 'Nobody comes up here,' Sir Alf said with blunt resignation. 'Never see anyone from one day to the next.' They went into the kitchen. 'Hope you don't mind, but I can manage better in here. Coffee?'

'Fine,' said John, uttering his first word. They sat at the large kitchen table. 'I'm sorry,' he continued. 'I'd no idea you were...' His words tailed off as he struggled for a tactful phrase.

'Disabled.'

'Well, err, aye, not many know.'

'Fell off this bleeding ladder, only three feet from the ground. I didn't break anything, just went numb from the waist down. Damaged a nerve, they said at the hospital. Sommat to do with the spine. They said the feeling would come back. But it's been getting on two years now, and, well, sod all... '

At this point, Flora pushed open the door and cut him short. Having heard all she wanted to hear, she thought it pointless to earwig any more. She curtsied, grinned, and in a mischievous voice asked, 'Will that be all, your lordship?'

Sir Alf, initially taken aback, turned to her and replied, 'Yes, Flora, that will be all till tomorrow.'

'I'll be off then.' She curtsied, turned and giggled as she left.

'You're not entirely alone then?' John was now aware that his friend's situation was not as dire as he made out.

'She's just the maid, housekeeper like. Goes round with the mop, nowt else,' said Sir Alf, attempting but failing to justify her presence. 'Now John, nice to see you, but I gather you've not come round here for the social. What can I do for you?'

John dropped his head. 'Well it's like this … we're not after charity or a donation … but up at the club, things are getting out of hand.'

'Good Jesus, how can running a cricket club get out of hand?'

'Well, we've had to respond to this ten-year rule of yours,' John said, raising his voice.

'Look, I know what you're thinking. I tried to get it stopped, but my lad had already sent out the letter. At present, he runs the show until I am back on me feet. Not the best arrangement, I'll grant you,' he half-apologised, and then turned the argument round. 'Point is, though, what the hell's going on up there? The rule was devised so that any tin-pot club could handle it. You only have to win a cup or sommat once in ten years. Not a lot to ask, is it?'

John rose to the defence of his colleagues and as he did, added grit to his voice. 'We put up with a lot of crap, we manage on minimum income and sod-all equipment. We put in loads of hours to keep the club fit for visitors. The players just play and piss off. Everyone thinks it looks after itself, well it doesn't, we do it – the committee.' He paused for breath then carried on. 'We've overlooked this soddin' rule of yours, but if someone else thinks they can do a better job, then let 'em try.' He stood up to leave.

'Hey, steady on, sit down,' Sir Alf responded, realising he had touched a nerve.

John calmed down, then went on. 'Your lad, he's mixed us a right bottle. We have no money. It's hand to mouth every week but to solve this problem, we've had to invest in this pro, and he is not cheap. Some money is coming in, but we need to pay some of his wages up front. Do you follow? No money, no pro, no pro, no win, no win, no cup … no cup, no club. Simple.'

Sir Alf scratched his head. 'No effing idea, if you ask me. How much are you short?'

'About two grand would tide us over,' John hissed through his teeth as he spoke.

Sir Alf fell back in his chair. 'Hell … things have changed. Who've you got – Richie bleeding Benaud?'

'Benjamin Saxon's his name.'

Sir Alf, slightly over-acting, looked at the ceiling. 'Jesus, have we none of our own who can do the business?'

'We would if we had, but we haven't,' John replied pointedly.

'Well it's a sad state… I'll see you get your two grand but it's only a loan, understand?'

John smiled. 'Thanks Alf, you're a good un.'

'Think I need sommat a bit stronger,' said Sir Alf peering into his empty cup.

John, now smiling even more broadly, did not need asking. 'You should get yourself to the club, we have the best ale in town. Sheep's Head it's called.'

As Sir Alf poured the drinks, his mind was racing in other directions: 'Two grand here, alterations to the chair and more cash for Flora. God's sake, best go see the man at Barclays… '

He looked up to see John looking at him expectantly. 'What's that, who's got a sheep's head?'

The Ram Inn

The refurbished and renamed Ram Inn now had a more relaxed atmosphere. Gone were the widescreen televisions on which the locals could watch sport. The old-fashioned jukebox had been replaced by mindless mood music.

'We're after a different type of clientele, more respectable and discerning … people with … taste,' said Ralph the new barman. He emphasised the point with a simpering smile, as if the person he was addressing did not fit the description.

'People with money, you mean,' chipped in a regular, clearly dissatisfied with the changes. 'Before you did it up, you could get a pint for less than a quid. I need a bleedin' mortgage for one now.'

'Ah but it's real ale now, it's been passed as excellent, we're in the *Better Beer Book*.' Ralph pointed to a certificate behind the bar.

'Passed by the management,' interrupted an irate customer.

'Pissed by them more like,' added another.

The customers' confidence in barracking the new barman grew. 'Sheep's Head? More like Sheep *Dip*,' shouted a man at the back.

The intensity rose.

'One pound effing fifty, for warm sheep's piss.'

'What the hell's going on?' It was the owner of the pub, Anthony Dawes; he had dashed in when he heard the racket.

'Nothing boss, just a bit of light-hearted banter,' Ralph replied with a wobble in his voice.

An anonymous heckler from the back added to Ralph's apparent lack of control. 'Banter, banter! You put our beer up by forty pee, then dish out this gnat's piss.'

Anthony stepped in. 'Gentlemen, gentlemen … please.' He gained their attention and then attempted to offset the disturbance. 'I'm sure you'll agree the place is much better since the modernisation, but we have to recover the costs.'

'More convivial,' interrupted Ralph.

'Keep out,' snapped Anthony, still maintaining a grin.

'Price's gone up and the beer's crap,' shouted a complainer from the back.

'Crap! Crap? I'll have you know, this ale is a prize winner.' Anthony grabbed the pump handle. He pulled the ale into a pint glass, but immediately became suspicious.

'What the…?' He was lost for words as he looked at the cloudy liquid in the glass. He sipped and gritted his teeth. 'Good Jesus,' he remarked, spitting it back into the glass. 'It's off!' He pulled another pint and sniffed it, then as the vinegary odour entered his nose he threw his head back. 'This is well off.' He looked down at the cooler switch beneath the bar, 'How long has this been off?'

Ralph began to colour up. 'Never been on. It's a cool day, didn't think you needed it.'

'You've been serving sour beer all day?' Ralph nodded. 'Change the barrel then apologise to all these folk. Give them their money back out of the till, and buy them a round out of your own pocket.'

Ralph nodded again. As he pulled the round, the pub echoed to the chant of, 'Easy, easy, easy.'

Roland, Joseph Lagg and the brothers Simon and Reginald of Jakeson & Jakeson Builders and Property

Repairers Inc had arranged to meet earlier, but were distracted by the commotion.

'So, what have you to report?' Roland asked impatiently.

'We've done as you asked, been round to his old club and snooped round,' replied Simon, demonstrating what he had done with a facial expression.

Roland rolled his eyes. 'Get on with it!' he barked.

'It seems he was very well liked, particularly by the women. He fathered a couple of kids by all accounts. Difficult to prove though, no one would commit themselves.'

Roland butted in with a confused expression. 'Excuse me! Difficult to prove? The guy's black, isn't he?'

They looked at him as though he were talking a foreign language. Realising this, he waved his hands in surrender, 'No, no, it doesn't matter now, you carry on.'

Simon took a deep breath. 'It were curious. Every club he's been to, they all say he can be relied on. Big Ben is like clockwork.'

Roland's patience was wearing thin. 'Yes, yes, OK, but is there anything we can make use of?'

'Not really, he's just a nice bloke. We've been to watch him. Can't half knock a ball, he won the game in the last over. Everyone were jumping up and down and screaming. They are doing well in the league now.'

Roland's anger boiled over. 'Great, just great! I send two men out to do a bit of undercover muckraking, and they turn out to be clowns having a jolly on my expenses. Well you'll have to do better than this. The idea was to find something we can use to scotch him. No muck, no pay.'

'Funny you should mention that,' said Reginald thoughtfully.

'What, muck?' snapped Roland, now raising his voice.

'No … scotch,' he continued. 'Seems he gets melancholy after a few whiskies, and then goes on a bender for days. He's been known to go missing all week. Don't turn up for matches, nothin'. All it takes is one glass to set him off. So they were all keen to keep him away from the top shelf.'

Roland leaned back into his chair and gave a wry smile. 'That's better,' he oozed.

Simon went to the bar flashing Roland's crisp ten-pound note like a trophy. The others remained in their seats, deep in thought. Roland leaned forward and whispered his proposal after the beer arrived. 'So all we have to do is get someone to get close to him, become his buddy. Then one Friday, buy him a few drinks – and bingo!'

They all looked at Joe. 'You can get stuffed if you think I'm doing your dirty work,' he rapped.

'Look,' Roland said softly, indicating that he did want Joe to do his dirty work. 'All you've got to do is get cosy with him. It's weeks away from any … dirty work.'

'Not happy, not happy' protested Joe.

The brothers sniggered.

'It's got to be a vital game, one that the league or a cup depends on. That's where you two come in,' instructed Roland.

In unison, the smirk fell from the brothers' faces. 'Us?' they protested.

'It's up to you two to figure out which game is the clincher. It'll have to be a home game and played on a Saturday. With a bit of luck, we will skittle him for the whole weekend. Two matches in one go.'

'Just like the little tailor,' chipped in Simon.

The others, bemused, stared at him blankly. Then Reginald, embarrassingly, offered an explanation. 'It were flies, and there were seven of them, you thick bastard.'

'Don't call me a thick bastard,' he shouted across the table.

'For God's sake sit down and keep quiet! This was supposed to be an inconspicuous meeting, not a bar-room brawl,' Roland hissed. 'Now, you know what you have to do?' They nodded in agreement. 'Just think of the holidays you can have after we pull this off. Now, anyone want a Sheep's Head?'

Reginald looked at Simon. 'I'm gonna have you outside...'

Saturday Morning:
Ready to Go

Geoffrey put on his coat and grabbed his car keys. He was almost ready to set off on another mission to try and get clubs to change their existing brewery to his. However, he paused and turned back up the hallway. He sensed a change but, not being able to put his finger on it, he offered simple but probing questions.

'What have you got on today? Shopping?'

'Done that,' said Susan.

'Did it yesterday,' confirmed Alison.

'Going to see your mum then?'

'No, not today.' Susan did not lift her eyes from the freezer box she was filling.

'Ah, going on a picnic?' he said confidently.

'Not exactly a picnic…'

'We're going to watch Benjamin,' said his daughter.

'We're going to the cricket,' Susan quickly interrupted. 'Strange as it may seem, we've less chance of being hit by the ball if we're at the ground.'

'Who's Benjamin?' asked Geoffrey.

'He's a big, big man,' giggled Alison.

'He's the professional at the cricket club,' Susan added with authority.

'He's ever so strong, he carried Mummy from the doorway and put her on the settee, just like she was a baby,' said Alison with mischief in her voice.

Geoffrey's face set in a glare. 'First I've heard of this, what's been going on?'

'Nothing's going on, it's a long story, I'll tell you later,' she said, still staring into the bottom of the freezer box in order to avoid eye contact. 'Look, we must go or we'll miss the toss,' she added, trying to put a stop to the topic.

Geoffrey scowled.

'I'll get an explanation from you later, do you hear?'

His voice tailed off as he stomped down the hallway and slammed the door. Seconds later, they heard the noise of a revving engine.

'Now see what you've done, you've made Daddy all upset,' Susan said as she screwed the top on the Thermos.

Sir Alf Ventures Out

The taxi approached the main street in the centre of Throttle. Here, large Victorian properties were interspersed with modern concrete shops. Sir Alf stared out of the taxi window. Although it had not been that long since he visited the place, he could have sworn it had changed.

'Don't recognise any of these shops,' he muttered to the back of the driver's head. The driver pulled up outside the bank. 'Just dump me here, I'll be all right.'

'You sure?' Sir Alf nodded impatiently and the driver rolled his eyes. 'Your funeral,' he coughed as he rummaged in the boot, then put down the steel ramps to the pavement.

'Here, keep the change.'

'Cheers,' said the driver in a voice that indicated his disgust at the twenty-pence tip. As the driver helped him out of the taxi, his face suddenly lit up. 'Knew I'd get it! You're Alfred Bullock, the mill owner.'

Sir Alf looked at him. 'I used to be, look at me now. Want to swap?'

'Not a chance,' the driver replied unkindly as he helped him down the ramp.

Sir Alf looked up at the bank. He had visited the place many times before, albeit not for a couple of years. Before, he had not noticed the large imposing doorway or the grand steps up to the entrance. As he sat in the wheelchair, it all looked much taller than before. All of a sudden, he felt helpless. Although it was not a hot day, beads of sweat began to form on his forehead. His mind raced back to the meetings he had attended here, important meetings.

He used to strut around in this place. The managers, and he had seen a few, would fawn over him because he had wealth, and wealth meant influence.

'And now I can't even get into the frigging place!' he shouted in despair.

A queue of people at the nearby bus stop turned and stared, but did not help. He felt embarrassed and angry. Then a voice from behind alerted him. 'Is it Mr Bullock?'

He looked up. At the top of the steps, a dark-suited young lady repeated the question. 'Mr Bullock, to see Mr Roscoe?' He nodded.   She skipped down the steps and grabbed the wheelchair handles. 'The disabled entrance is round the corner,' she said, urging him on.

'I am not disabled,' he advised sternly. 'Just a temporary problem with me legs, and I am quite capable of operating this chair on me own.' Seconds later, he gripped the sides of the wheels and stopped. 'Young lady,' he said, but now in a softer voice tinged with remorse.

'Call me Linda,' she replied.

'Linda, I'm sorry, it's just that I used to stride in here without a second's thought, but now it's a major operation.'

She smiled. 'No problem, this way Mr Bullock.'

Humbled, he thought, 'What a miserable thing to do.'

Once inside, she pushed him towards a large oak-panelled door and gently knocked; seconds later, the door opened.

'Sorry I'm late, I couldn't find the entrance,' Sir Alf apologised.

'No problem at all. You are right about the ramp. Planners would not let us put it at the front, they said it would ruin the façade,' said Mr Roscoe.

Sir Alf looked round the bank manager's office. Gone were the leather chair and dark oak desk with inkstands.

These had been replaced with soft furnishings and a computer on the end of a semi-circular, plastic-topped unit.

'Curious that you should make an appointment today,' Roscoe said casually, bringing Sir Alf back to the point of the visit.

'Oh, why's that?'

'We had your Roland in here only last week. Milk with your coffee?' he asked as Linda rattled down the cups.

Sir Alf gripped the sides of his chair. 'Our Roland, what did he want?'

Mr Roscoe looked at him sideways. 'Surely you know? The loan for the new development?'

'Company's well off with all the income from the units,' Alf said, beginning to get worked up.

There was a pause as Mr Roscoe rattled the keys of the computer, then stared at the screen. He leaned back in his chair, raised his eyebrows and pointed with an open palm to the screen. 'I'm afraid at present the income barely covers the outgoings. I'm sorry to say that between the two directors, Miriam and Roland, most of the income is spent.'

Sir Alf went quiet; he took his time as he dunked a biscuit in his coffee. 'Keep calm, keep calm,' he told himself. 'Right Mr Roscoe. Yes, of course, the proposed new development. Still at the feasibility stage… Anyway, I could do with a few quid for my personal use, about five grand should cover it.'

'No problem Mr Bullock, peanuts compared to four hundred and fifty thousand pounds.'

Sir Alf's cup wobbled on the saucer. 'Four hundred and fifty…'

'Apparently, the scheme to redevelop the cricket ground will cost at least that. Of course, if all the houses are sold above their target price, you should more than double your investment.'

Sir Alf went cold; not for a long while had he experienced so many emotions in such a short time.

'And can I advise you, that for a man of your integrity, it isn't necessary to make an appointment to withdraw five thousand pounds. Just give the bank a ring and we will have it ready for you. Is there anything else I can help you with?'

Sir Alf shook his head, but not in reply to the question. Moments later Sir Alf, plus bulging brown envelope in his inside pocket, found himself on the pavement outside.

'Be all right, will you, Mr Bullock?' said Linda. She had lowered her voice to avoid drawing unnecessary attention.

'I think so,' he mouthed. His mind still racing, he set off to find Cargill & Sons Solicitors.

At home he was used to having unhindered access when moving about. Ramps, widened doorways and a lift had been installed so he could move around freely. However, negotiating the pavements and crossing the roads was a new experience. There were people in the way, prams, dogs, lamp-posts, telephone boxes. Crossing the road became a life-threatening matter. He gasped as huge lorries passed within inches. 'The bastards aren't even slowing down,' he muttered to himself at the kerb edge. He looked up and down the street. 'Bloody hell,' he said aloud as a van nearly wiped him out.

He was just about to try again when he was rescued by a familiar voice. 'Need a lift?'

He turned to see the taxi driver leaning out of his cab window. 'If you don't mind,' he said, panting.

'Different world isn't it? My old man used to get so screwed up when he went out in his chair,' said the driver, opening the cab door. 'Where to?'

'Cargill & Sons Solicitors.'

'Good job I came along,' laughed the driver. 'It's the other end of town. You'd have been ages.'

Sir Alf took a deep breath. 'Got to sort this out … all of it.' He pondered his plight for a moment and depression came over him.

The driver, however, had his own opinion. 'You've got it easy,' he announced. 'Big house, plenty of helpers and cash.' Sir Alf's jaw fell open. 'My old man used to work in your mill before you had it!' said the driver, partially turning his head. 'His insides got so clogged up with the fluff he hadn't the breath to walk. We pushed him for miles in his chair, trying to get some fresh air into him. He died about ten years ago.'

Sir Alf was trying to think of a suitable reply. Luckily the speed of the taxi saved him from the quandary.

'Do you want me to wait?' asked the driver.

'Best not, no knowing how long I'll be,' Alf replied, choosing his words carefully. 'But you can help me inside, if you will.'

Once inside, he found himself looking up at another high counter. 'Is Terry Cargill in?' he said.

'I'll just see if he can be disturbed,' said the receptionist peering down at him and using an affected plummy voice. 'What is it about?' she enquired, following orders from her boss to protect him from timewasters.

'That's between me and him,' Sir Alf barked, leaving no doubt that it was a private matter.

Startled, she wondered if it was worth her pittance of a wage having to deal with this kind of confrontation. She sniffed the air, looked down her nose, turned and entered the door marked Private.

Sir Alf heard her, now speaking in her regional accent, ranting through the gap left by the automatic door. 'If you think I'm putting up with this crap all the time...'

He smiled and wheeled himself over to the waiting area. He picked up a magazine. No sooner had he opened it than a voice from the old days enveloped him. 'Alf, how are you? Sorry for ... you know what I mean...' He was staring at the wheelchair. 'Come in, for goodness' sake. Agnes, make us a brew, it's one of my old mates.'

Sir Alf was right not to keep the taxi driver waiting. The pleasantries, the tea and biscuits, and finally the reminiscences, all took more than an hour.

'What brings you here? Surely not just passing?' Terry said, looking at the clock and realising the time.

'It's confidential. I need your help, but I also need your word it won't go any further.'

Terry swung his chin from side to side as he straightened his tie, a mannerism that Sir Alf suddenly remembered. 'We go back a long way, you and me, and if we can't help each other in a crisis, it's a poor do.'

'Well it's our Roland, he's about as much idea as- '

'I'd heard whispers,' butted in Terry.

'Whispers, what whispers?'

'It's difficult to say, they're only rumours,' hedged Terry.

'Come on, out with it!'

'Well, he's getting himself in a bit of a mess, not to mention mixing with a few, how can we say, less than straight individuals.'

'For Christ's sake, Terry, speak your mind.'

'Here it is then, as much as I know. Apparently, the books are not balancing as they should… You know, the recession … its hit many folk hard, particularly the one-man bands who rent small units. You do know that half your units are empty?'

'No.'

'So the income is halved, but Roland still has his new Jag and posh living. From what I hear, he's trying to borrow his way out of trouble. I tell you, if it goes pear-shaped, he'll take you with him.'

Sir Alf stared forwards but did not focus. His mind was racing back over the past twenty years of graft and deals; he thought he had handed over a doddle of a job to his son. 'Take the rent, install a new tenant. Take the rent, install new tenant – that's all he has to do. What could be simpler?' he thought.

'All that time building it up and in less than three years he's made a balls of it.'

'He doesn't keep you in touch then?' sympathised Terry.

'Not a word, thought everything was going OK,' winced Sir Alf.

'We thought you knew… '

'I've got to get back in control. Can you give us a hand?'

'I'll do what I can. We all thought you were a bit hasty handing it over like you did. Office boy to chairman! He won't be easy to shift.'

'My fault really, thought he could handle it. With my accident an' all, I weren't thinking straight.'

Terry tried to cheer him up. 'I'll do some checking, I'm sure we can sort it out… Agnes, can you call a cab?'

Sir Alf smiled, 'Remember the one that fetched me?'

'Yes, Rally Cabs, I think it was,' Agnes said.

'Any but that.'

Susan and a Quandary

Susan was part way through the drudge of house cleaning. However, on this particular day she had her mind on other things. Thoughts kept getting in the way of her doing her usual just acceptable effort at keeping the house ready to be wrecked and soiled again. She switched off the noisy vac and sat on the edge of the bed, pondering the last few days and wondering how life could get so complicated.

'One minute everything's hunky-dory, the next all hell breaks loose. Here I am, so-called happily married, daughter healthy and normal, nice house – albeit in the firing line of the cricket, husband with a reasonably secure job. So why ruin it all? Why risk all this for that?'

These thoughts went through her mind as she caught sight of Benjamin going round and round the cricket pitch on the motor mower. He had agreed to complete this time-consuming task as the club was short of volunteers. 'All I have to do is sit here,' he said.

Susan moved to the window and pulled up the little padded chair that usually sat in front of the dresser. Elbows on the sill and head in hands, she asked herself, 'What is it? Infatuation, lust, desire? I don't fancy him like you fancy a hunk on the telly, and it's not love.' Nevertheless, whatever 'it' was, it made her uneasy, unable to relax. 'It' was always on her mind. 'It' bugged her.

'So what is it?' she shouted, as her eyes followed the mower on its tighter and tighter route to the centre of the pitch. She loved Geoffrey and they had a sex life. 'So,' she pondered, 'what's going to be different?'

This she did not know. One thing she did know was that, as soon as she caught sight of Benjamin, her breathing rate increased, her legs went to jelly and she began to feel hot. In fact, she was sweating now. Having recently read self-help books entitled, *How to Be Assertive*, immediately followed by *Feel the Fright and Do It Anyway*, she felt it her duty to go and get whatever she desired. In her own words, 'Hang the consequences.' This phrase echoed back moments later when she thought about the sentences handed out to adulterous wives in the Far East. She took a deep breath. 'But that is there and this is here, and I'm not getting any younger.'

So that was it: she had to know what it was that nearly poked her eye out when she had come to her senses on the settee that fated Saturday afternoon. She stood up just in time catch a rear view of Benjamin as he drove the mower into the shed.

'You're only here once! And Benjamin is only here another fifteen weeks, so I'd better get my skates on.'

As she made her way downstairs, she began to plot. 'Mmm, got to get closer, need an excuse, a reason for being there.'

She arrived in the kitchen and added several words to the bottom of the shopping list. *Cricket rules. Cricket ground maintenance. Running a committee.*

'That should do for starters.'

The Go-Faster Wheelchair

Sir Alf was mulling over his new problems when the phone rang.

'Tom Reagan here... your chair, I've made it better, don't half go. It's ready. Can I bring it round?'

'Of course you can … I'm in all day.' Sir Alf sighed. He put the phone down, but spoke as if there was still someone there. 'Be glad of a distraction, take my mind off everything else.'

It did not seem long before the front doorbell rang.

'You must have been phoning from the end of the drive.'

'Why … what do you mean?'

Sir Alf began to realise that maybe it was his daydreaming that had caused the confusion. 'You'll have to excuse me, I'm having an off day.'

'Nobody's perfect,' Tom retorted in an unsympathetic huff.

Sir Alf threw out a lifeline: 'Let's start again, would you like a coffee?'

'That'd be grand. I'll be getting it out of the van.'

Sir Alf smiled and wheeled into the kitchen. Five minutes later, he returned balancing a tray. As soon as he saw the new chair his jaw dropped in amazement. 'Eeee … that looks … bloody excellent!' he said with obvious delight.

'I've done some extra mods.'

'You've done what?' replied Sir Alf, whilst running his fingers near a vertical handle with a red top.

'Don't touch that!' Tom shouted. 'It'll be off like a shot if you move that.'

Sir Alf pulled back his arm as though he had received an electric shock. 'Are you sure this is going to be all right?' he winced.

'You'll get used to it. Now, about these mods, err … alterations,' Tom said, trying to reduce the jargon. 'First off, it's a lot, lot faster. It has four high-revving instant-response motors, four-wheel drive, if you like. The power will come in smooth if you want or all at once, because of this power actuator.'

'Throttle,' said Sir Alf.

'What?' replied Tom.

'Throttle, it's a bleeding throttle.'

Tom ignored him and carried on enthusiastically. 'The steering has an improved lock, it has bigger and wider tyres.' At this point, he had to restrain himself from pointing at the wheels. 'Lights, indicators and a horn. What do you think of the seat?' He smiled, squeezing the leather upholstery. 'I got it out of an old Mini Cooper, complete with full race harness.'

Sir Alf stared. 'Seem to remember fighter pilots had these during the War!'

Undeterred by Sir Alf's comment, Tom ploughed on. 'If you're going off-road, it's a good idea to have one of these,' he pointed towards the cardboard box alongside the chair. Sir Alf reached inside and removed a shiny red crash helmet. 'I checked with the police. They say it's not compulsory, just a good idea.'

The expression on Sir Alf's face indicated that things were getting out of hand.

'Just wait till you try it! I have had endless fun testing it. Oh, just one thing …' Tom added. 'The police did say that if you exceed the speed limit, you'll be in a bit of bother, so go easy till you get used to it.'

'Really?' Sir Alf replied, warming to the idea.

'Oh aye, we've not had it flat out – couldn't find a road long enough. These motors will rev up to nine thousand rpm. That's fifty-odd miles an hour.'

'Hell fire!' Sir Alf said, a hint of excitement creeping into his voice.

'Now then, this clock tells you how much battery you've got left. As soon as you move, it starts ticking away. The faster you go, the faster the clock ticks, get it?'

Sir Alf stared at the gleaming paint and racing seat. Inside, he was aching to have a go. 'What do I owe you?'

'Four hundred and fifty quid for the parts,' said Tom, handing him an invoice.

'And the labour?' Sir Alf asked.

'Forget that, just sort out your lad.' Tom climbed into his van and wound down the window. 'Any problems, give us a bell. Oh, and don't forget the hat.'

Sir Alf had not been this excited since … well, he could not remember when. Within minutes he had swapped chairs, adjusted the seat belt and, although he did not think it necessary, had put on the helmet just to see what it felt like. Hesitantly, he turned the key and gently pushed forward the lever; he heard the motors whine as the chair edged forward.

'Bloody hell,' he muttered inside the helmet.

That afternoon he explored the whole grounds and beyond. He found places he had long forgotten and places within easy reach that he had never seen. As he located wooded glades and open views across the valley, Miriam's words came back to haunt him: 'Too busy looking after your soddin' mill…' Maybe if we had gone on walks together, things would have been different, he pondered.

Coming back up the drive, he looked at the clock. 'Loads of time left,' he thought. 'Let's see what it can do.'

He pushed the lever forward to its maximum. Gravel flew from behind each wheel and his head was thrown back. As the wheels fought for traction, the chair veered from side to side. He had to fight the steering to keep it in the centre of the drive. Seconds later, he came to a screeching halt as the hydraulic disc brakes locked up each wheel. He flicked up the visor, excitement coursing through him. He sat for a moment then undid the strap and lifted off the helmet. He did not know whether to laugh or cry. His heart pounded so loud he could hear it. He looked down and saw his hands trembling. 'Get a grip,' he urged himself.

He always considered himself to be in control. Even after the accident, visitors were impressed that he took the news of his impending confinement 'like a man'. His present condition was, he considered, totally out of character. Tears were not in his make-up, but he could not control himself. He had a lump in his throat and his eyes watered. He took out his hanky and blew his nose with a shaky hand.

'Can't be seen like this,' he chided himself, even though the possibility of anyone calling was remote. After a minute or so, he calmed down. He looked at the battery clock, then wiped it with his hanky. 'Another four hours left. I'll just have a brew and then I'll test it again.'

Dusk

As the light faded, Geoffrey Perkins checked all the doors on his car. It was not the first time he had been out; only an hour earlier he could have been seen pulling at the handles. He blamed this apparent loss of memory on a continuous alcohol intake.

'As a salesperson, I'm expected to demonstrate just how good my product is, a cross I must honourably bear in order to feed my wife and child,' he rambled as he re-entered the kitchen.

'What are you wittering about?' asked Susan at the sink.

'More meetings than NATO,' he replied.

'Where?' she said, turning and dripping water on the floor.

'Over there, men in suits, entering the club.' He pointed out of the window towards the clubhouse.

Susan's inquisitive nature got the better of her. She put on her shoes and went down the driveway. Geoffrey followed her.

'See!' he said, as a steady stream of well-dressed men knocked on the door, surreptitiously looked around, and then quickly entered. 'Something's going on up there, and it's not bingo.'

'Your suspicious mind will get you in trouble one of these days,' Susan mused. She returned to the kitchen and immersed her hands in what was now cold dishwater.

Miriam Escapes to Be Pampered

Miriam was relaxing at her favourite health club on the first day of a long weekend break. Having just had a sauna, she was now in the cooling-off area, reclining on a wicker lounger wearing a white towelling robe. She watched the other women dipping into the plunge bath and then going back to the sauna. To her amazement, some did not bother with robes. 'Your body's got to be perfect to do that, and some clearly aren't,' she thought as a middle-aged woman, who obviously could not have cared less, wobbled by.

She closed her eyes to the view and tried to relax. But things, personal things, were on her mind. 'Plenty of money, no need to work, I should be ecstatic. So why am I not?' She could not decide whether life was treating her badly. True, she was well off, but it had not gone as planned.

Her beginnings were humble and, as a child, she had always wondered what it would be like to be rich. It seemed curious now, but the only jobs open to her when she was about to leave school were in the mill. By the time she left, however, the mills had shut. She ended up serving dinners at the local chip shop instead.

Unaware of his intentions, she served plain Alf Bullock for months before he got up the courage to ask her out. She had always dreamt of a whirlwind romance but settled for being courted amidst the smell of hot fat and vinegar. Everyone thought she was so lucky to be chosen by the owner of the mill.

In those days, life was a dream – from chip shop server to boss's girlfriend in one fell swoop. Big cars became the norm, as did holidays down south.

After the wedding, reality dawned and the novelty began to wear a bit thin. She thought that Roland's arrival would provide her with the purpose in life she so dearly needed. It did for the first few years, until his father decided that Roland should go away for his education. At the tender age of four, Roland was dragged away from his mother's embrace and packed off to prep school. With him went Miriam's motherhood and enthusiasm. For the first term that Roland was away, she was depressed. She could not understand why her husband had insisted on sending the boy away when clearly she needed him with her. From that point, cracks appeared in their marriage. Now, as she looked back, she realised she had never really loved Alf in the first place. It was his money and lifestyle she loved, but now she hated them.

The final straw came as she held out her arms to welcome her son after only one term at boarding school. He had changed. His accent was all posh and he continually criticised her for 'talking common'. Mummy's boy had become a brat.

Whilst Roland was away at school and Alf was working, Miriam spent a lot of time on her own in the house. It was after yet another idle day, flicking through magazines designed for women with time on their hands, that she discovered what she thought would be an interest. This would not only help her get over the disappointment at home, but might also give her a much-needed direction. She decided it was time to smarten the place up. 'Give me an excuse to invite folk over, have some parties,' she dreamed.

She got in interior designers and had the place totally redecorated: flock wallpaper, fancy coving, brash curtains, dado rails, swags and tails. 'The business,' as she put it. Sir Alf, with his usual disapproval, commented: 'Put me *out of* bleeding business, the cost of all this.'

To a degree, it worked. They had parties but they were not the type of social gatherings Miriam had envisaged, more friends coming for a nosy at the decor. The majority thought it brassy and usually ended up drifting to the pub.

Since the accident and, as a consequence, the destruction of all her efforts to make the house fit for publication in *Up North Life*, she had lost all interest in the house. The thought of what Alf might wreck in her absence made her reluctant to return home. The role of wife and mother had become a sham, a token gesture; she was just going through the motions.

She even went through the night-class routine, thinking she would latch on to something arty or creative but nothing grabbed her. The nearest she came was aromatherapy; she really enjoyed that till she was asked to give a massage to a person she described as 'wrinkly'. It put her off so much, she didn't return.

She was in a quandary. 'I need a purpose and an objective. In the short term, I need the money to find an objective, but to keep the cash flowing I have to be part of the Bullock family. Jesus, what a mess, there has to be an answer.' The thoughts ran riot in her head. She had considered getting a divorce, even gone to the front door of the solicitors, and then walked away. Just the thought of the upheaval was enough to put her off, and being presented with a lump sum was like being made redundant. She'd probably blow it all in one go. The record went round and round. 'No purpose, not happy, but plenty of cash, no purpose, not happy, but plenty of cash, no…'

A soft male voice interrupted her thoughts, releasing her from her torment. 'Time for the next stage, Mrs Bullock. Are you ready?'

She opened her eyes and stared straight at the source of the request, a squeaky-clean young man with a beaming smile. 'You're dead right I am, love,' she replied.

Mid-Season Meeting

John Appleby coughed throatily and waved his agenda to bring the meeting to order.

'Can I welcome you all to the fifth meeting of the season? I'd like to offer a particularly warm welcome to a new member, Mrs Susan Perkins. Good to have you on board, we're always grateful for an extra pair of hands.'

Susan exchanged courteous glances with the other members.

'We've met before though, haven't we?' chipped in Tom Deakin. 'You came to the karaoke night with your Geoffrey. He's the one who supplied the ale that night.'

The others nodded, apart from Janice who just gritted her teeth.

'I couldn't stop long – babysitter problems – but I heard it was a success,' Susan enthused.

'Depends on how you rate success,' Janice spat. 'If you rate it on how much cleaning up you have to do afterwards, it were a roaring success. I can only say it's the last time I man the mop-bucket. It were days before I stopped heaving and the smell...' To emphasise the point, she screwed up her face as though she had just bitten into a lemon.

'Yes, yes, thank you for that personal observation, Janice, but we must move on,' interjected John.

Wanting to put an end to the subject, Susan completed her prepared acceptance speech. 'Thank you for the warm welcome. I look forward to assisting the committee members in their endeavour to ensure the survival of the club.' Silently she added what she really meant to say, 'and the opportunity of engaging in a bit of self-indulgence.'

John Appleby went on. 'That reminds me, I've had a letter from the brewery congratulating us on the condition of our pumps. They say that if we need any help, we-'

'Point of order, Mr Chairman,' said Susan, interrupting him.

He looked over his glasses: 'Yes?'

'Surely this item comes under the section of correspondence during the secretary's report?'

'Yes, but I thought it was relevant,' said John, taken aback.

'It might be relevant, but it's definitely correspondence.' Janice smirked as she spoke.

John looked at the others for support. They shrugged their shoulders.

'Susan's right,' added Tom mischievously.

'Well I think it's nit-picking, supposed to be a friendly, social type of committee.'

John, having taken umbrage, straightened his tie and then his glasses. He cleared his throat and added, 'Anybody else wants to do this pigging job, they're welcome.'

Janice, who did not get that many opportunities to stick the knife in, continued, 'It's not that we don't want you to continue. It's just that if a job's worth doing, it's worth doing right...' She looked down at her lap to hide her smile but failed.

'Can I move progress, Mr Chairman, else I'm going to bugger off home,' interrupted Fred in a much louder voice than usual.

'Hear, hear,' added Tom, not wanting to be left out.

'Very well, can we have the secretary's report, please?' John sat down in a huff.

Arthur trudged his way through his list of items, until he reached an issue that fell right into Susan's lap. 'We're about a third of the way through the season. We could do with a quick appraisal of what we need to get us through the next third, a simple inventory. We are OK in the kitchen, that takes care of itself. It's the other bits and bobs – cleaning, toiletries – and making sure we've got enough stuff in the shed.'

'You mean whitening, loam, grass seed, and petrol for the mower,' Susan said authoritatively. The others were shocked into silence.

'Yes, well … er … aye, that sort of stuff,' stuttered Arthur.

'No problem,' said Susan. 'Just make a list, I'll do the rest. I don't mind, so long as you don't want it right away. I can pop across whenever I've got a spare moment.' Her calm exterior belied the excitement building up inside her.

'Fine, that's all sorted then,' said John. 'I'll put it in the minutes then it's done proper. Susan to do inventory…' he said as he wrote.

'Can I have the treasurer's report please?'

Fred asserted himself. 'It's been a complicated period. All of a sudden, we are very well off. However, I must warn the committee that it is a false picture. We started at the beginning of the season with a deficit of fifty-six pounds. We now have over two thousand pounds in the bank after paying Benjamin his wages. But I have to tell you that the money is a loan from Sir Alfred Bullock.'

The committee members, apart from John and Susan, gasped.

'If I could come in here,' said John getting quickly to his feet. 'Fred and I had a quick look at the books and it was quite clear that we weren't going to make it through the first month, let alone the season. We needed some cash in hand. So I took it on myself to sort it out. Alf Bullock is an old friend who has offered us cash when we were hard up before. On this occasion, we decided it was in the club's best interest to accept his offer. If we lost Benjamin because we could not pay him, we would be knackered for the rest of the season. Don't forget we need to win something.' John paused.

A silence suggested indecision in the minds of the rest of the committee. Susan looked round and sensed the dilemma. 'Well, I'd like to offer my thanks to John and Fred who have used their initiative to prevent the potential closure of the club.'

The others, grateful for the direction, followed suit. 'Yes, yes, well done,' they added, stopping just short of cheering.

When the plaudits had ceased, Janice raised her hand. 'It's right to praise them but what I can't understand is how, after all the wages have been paid and all the other expenditure, we still have so much money in the bank. All we've had is one karaoke night and borrowed two thousand pounds.'

Fred leapt in. 'I'll gladly go through the accounts with you,' he offered, in the hope that she would decline. 'It's very complex and this is neither the time nor the place. But I can assure you that all is in order.'

'It's not that I don't trust you, Fred … I'd trust you with my last penny … it's just that in simple maths…'

Fred stopped her: 'We made more on the karaoke than we first thought, Janice. It's as simple as that, OK?' He raised his voice slightly.

Janice noted his manner and backed down. 'Sure, glad we've so much.'

'That's the end of my report, Mr Chairman. Now, if we can move on, I have to go shortly.'

The others stared at Fred. His raised voice was now accompanied by a twitch below his right eye.

'He's lying,' thought Susan.

No one had the heart for any other business, and the meeting broke up quickly. Susan accompanied Janice through the door. 'Never seen Fred like that before,' Janice muttered as soon as the door shut behind them.

Inside, John, Fred and Tom remained at the bar. They waited until the click of the gate indicated they could not be overheard. 'Well done Fred, she never suspected a thing,' said Tom grinning.

Fred did not quite see it that way. 'This is a right how-do-you-do,' he replied, getting angrier. 'You've got me falsifying the books, lying to Janice and lying to my wife. If she finds out, I'm dead meat.'

Tom looked at him. 'What are you lying about to your wife?'

'I told her it was darts and dominoes. I couldn't have come otherwise.'

'You didn't mention the stripper then,' said John, digging Fred in the ribs as he spoke.

'That's another thing! You lot lied. "Exotic dancer, just like a disco," you said.'

'Bet you didn't know where to look,' laughed John as the humour gained pace.

Tom put on a straight face and confronted the others. 'That bloody snake had me worried. Big bugger. What would we have done if that had got loose?'

'Sent for Janice, she'd have seen it off,' roared John.

'Anyway, let's get down to brass tacks. How much did we make?' asked Tom.

Fred's face cracked a smile mixed with resignation. 'It were a bit awkward to work out. Seemed to be money coming from all angles, nobody kept a check on how many tickets we sold. I was just given a bag of cash marked "tickcts". I asked some if they'd paid, and they said they didn't know but they were quite happy to pay again. Football cards going round all night, profit from the bar, made a fortune there.' He paused for a moment and the others looked at him expectantly.

'Strangest thing though, I found this old bucket with the stripper's name on it. Mainly pound coins … over a hundred quid when I counted it. As she was leaving, I asked her if she wanted it. She said she'd taken all the notes but had a reputation to maintain, said she wouldn't be seen dead walking the streets with a bucket of loose change.'

The others roared with laughter. 'What's so funny?' Fred asked. The others were too busy holding their stomachs or wiping away the tears to reply. 'Anyway, we made over five hundred quid on the night,' he went on proudly.

'Bucket of loose change,' spluttered John.

Opportunity Knocks for Susan

Benjamin had risen, as usual, just after noon. Still in a fog from the previous night's excesses, he made his way to the cricket ground. He had a list of ground maintenance chores to perform and so within minutes of arrival, he was lazily going round and round the pitch, sitting on the motor mower and moving his head rhythmically to the music playing on his headphones.

Susan, in the hallway of her house, was staring at the mirror, psyching herself up for the next phase of her quest. 'No need for excuses, I have an official reason for being there. The sun is shining and so am I,' she said confidently. She palmed her shorter-than-usual skirt down and raised her shoulders. 'Ready,' she added as she shut the door behind her and purposefully strutted towards the cricket ground.

She stood on the perimeter of freshly cut grass, took a deep breath and waited for Benjamin to make his way round to her side of the pitch. As he approached, she pretended to write in a spiral-bound notepad. She beckoned officiously as he got nearer. He veered off his route and came to rest alongside her. He cut the engine of the mower and removed his headphones.

'Afternoon, Mrs Perkins. Is it a good day or what?' he greeted her buoyantly, not really expecting an answer to his question.

She couldn't stop herself looking him over. She usually saw him at a distance in cricket whites but all he had on was a sloppy T-shirt, cut-off jeans and a pair of old sandals. Her heart pounded and she felt a droplet of perspiration make its way between her shoulder blades and down the small of her back. 'No backing out now,' she urged herself.

As he got closer, she stared at his big eyes, pearly-white teeth and a beaming smile. Beads of sweat like precious stones glistened on his dark forehead. She felt her heart palpitate. His rippling muscles flexed as he climbed down off the mower.

'Good God,' she muttered as she noted his huge hand deftly turn off his Walkman and remove his earplugs.

'Is you alright?' she heard him ask.

'Sorry … err … yes,' she stammered.

'You seemed gone for a minute,' he added, smiling.

She looked up at him. The sun was behind him, and it got in her eyes. She held her palm up to shield her face. 'I was wondering if you could help.'

'You name it.'

'I've been asked to do an inventory of the old store. Could you help me to identify some items? Won't take a minute,' she said, hoping the well-rehearsed lines did not sound too wooden.

'Sure can, anything to keep me off that old mower. It shakes my bones to bits,' he said as he rummaged in his pocket. 'I got the key right here.' He held out a well-used key dangling from a piece of frayed string.

They walked in silence to the white concrete garage that had adopted the name 'old store'. He opened the side door and let Susan in first. It was darker than she thought: what light there was came from whitewashed windows along one side.

'Can you see OK, Mrs Perkins, or shall I open the main door?'

'No!' she shouted, louder than she meant to. He looked at her, taken by surprise at the volume of her voice. 'It'll be fine when our eyes get adjusted,' she said more softly, with just a hint of apology.

They stood for a moment. Then, as their vision improved, he asked, 'What's first on your list then?' He screwed up his eyes to assist his vision.

'Grass seed,' she replied, putting down the pad on a sack that had grass seed on the label.

As he rooted among the other sacks, she moved over and gingerly closed the door. She had not reckoned on the metallic click of the latch. 'Hey, I can't see at all now,' he announced, unaware of her intentions. He turned to investigate and found Susan had moved over to him and was unbuttoning the top of her summer dress. Anticipating her intentions, he protested.

'Stop right there, Mrs Perkins, we're getting into very dangerous territory.' There was genuine fear in his voice.

'I'll take full responsibility for any consequences,' she whispered in an even softer tone.

Susan moved closer and took his hand. She was surprised how calm she was and how much he was trembling. He flinched as though it was too hot to touch. 'Relax,' she encouraged. She let go of his hand and undid the remainder of the buttons.

'We've got big, big problems if we gets caught,' he cautioned. The beads of sweat on his forehead multiplied. 'My job, your marriage and bad, bad publicity, have you thought this out?'

'I've thought about nothing else,' she said, taking control. 'Don't worry Benjamin, nobody's going to find out.' She sensed that he was beginning to tremble a little less.

'This is fire we're playing with,' he pleaded. 'Don't do it,' he muttered, weakening.

'No need to worry. I won't tell if you don't,' she added as her excitement increased.

***

Some time later, after Susan had showered, she wrapped her towelling robe around her and watched him through the bedroom window. He was tidying up the equipment, having marked out the pitch. He showed no outward sign of the past hour's goings-on, he just carried on nodding his head to the music as if nothing had happened.

Her head was still spinning, though. 'Bloody brilliant,' she whispered. 'Guilt? Mmmm, none so far…'

As she watched him load the wheelbarrow, she kept reliving the details of the afternoon. 'And all in proportion,' she giggled. Then within seconds, the smile faded from her face. 'Where does this leave me now? What about Geoffrey? Will I ever want him again? In some respects, I'm worse off.' She sat on the edge of the bed, thinking about her predicament.

She faced the mirror on the wardrobe door and confided, 'He was so strong, but unbelievably gentle. Never once did I think he would rush. Not like Geoffrey - all rough and tumble and smelling of beer - with the statutory "Have you finished yet?" at the end.' She kept looking at the mirror, half expecting to get an answer. She recalled how it used to be with Geoffrey. 'It hasn't always been bad. He was a good lover. What the hell's happened?' She turned away from the mirror and lay back on the bed. Her mind, like a video, rewound and fast-forwarded.

'What now? Can't leave it like this. I know it's risky but … well, it was so… good. And it can only get better, can't it?' She shuddered as she went through it again.

'Seriously, unbelievably, very good.'

A Neighbourly Drink

Geoffrey Perkins and Albert Bradley had not been neighbours long, but they had much in common. Each had concluded that living on the edge of Throttle's cricket pitch was a mistake – and it had, as the experience of the recent weeks had shown, become intolerable. They had assessed their own circumstances and decided that moving house would involve a considerable financial loss.

On the domestic front, each had tasks to perform that had been pleasures at first. But as time wore on, the novelty faded and the tasks became tedious chores. Since the removal of his beloved garden, Albert had replaced most of the plants with plastic replicas. He had installed hanging baskets on the edge of his guttering, where he thought the ball could not possibly reach. These initially overflowed with fuchsias, geraniums and other flowering species that in the past he could have cultivated with little or no bother at all but, by their very nature, hanging baskets require continuous attention. After suffering the rigours of the northern climate for a short time, they began to look tired and bedraggled. In an effort to maintain the correct moisture content and to ease the physical effort of lugging buckets of water up ladders, Albert installed a piped watering system to each plant. The pleasure of a job well done gave way to utter despair during subsequent test runs. The first plant on the piped run was deluged with water but the last only received drips. 'Despondent' was becoming a word he used frequently.

Next door, Geoffrey was out retrieving the day's playthings from the unkempt garden. He observed the scattered remains of extortionately priced toys, abandoned as though they were worthless. The cost of items had always been a source of interest to Geoffrey; he could relate the once much-sought-after items to the amount of hours he worked or how many barrels of beer he would have to sell. He looked down at a pair of once smart-looking trainers.

'Full morning's work there,' he muttered as he tugged them from a patch of long grass.

As he walked round putting the broken or out-of-favour toys into a large washing basket, he noticed Albert. He was sitting on the flagstones leading to his garden with his head between his hands. He also noticed water flooding from the hanging baskets to one side of his house.

'You look like you could do with a beer,' Geoffrey said as a thin stream of water made a direct path towards Albert, who leapt up as he felt the dampness creep through his trousers.

'Soddin' hell!'

'A beer – do you want one or what?' Geoffrey repeated, but louder.

'Yes, please.' Albert twisted his neck to look at the dark stain on his pants. Then he stared at the array of beers in the boot of Geoffrey's car. His eyes darted from one decoratively labelled bottle to another. 'I've never seen these before.'

Geoffrey explained the line of products. 'I'd value your opinion,' he lied.

They sat on Geoffrey's steps to avoid the soil and plant-laden stream that continued to pour down the front of

Albert's house. As the sun began to set, and the alcohol began to take effect, they mellowed.

'Wife will think I've pissed myself,' Albert grinned, looking at the contrasting colour on the back of his pants. There was a pause as his face slid back into a sombre expression. 'Soddin' nightmare out here, no peace at weekends,' he moaned.

'Not much we can do though,' sighed Geoffrey.

'Not exactly true – not now that your missus is in with them,' Albert replied with a slight slur.

'What do you mean?'

'I just heard that she's joined the committee,' said Albert, choosing his words more carefully and wondering why he had a problem pronouncing 'committee'.

'My wife's offered to help, that's all, make tea and sandwiches. Nowt wrong with that, is there?'

'You mean she's not trying to *infiltrate* them?' said Albert, winking strangely.

'Infiltrate! She's not a bleeding spy, she just wants to help out,' Geoffrey responded, trying not to raise his voice.

'Don't get me wrong, it's just that it'd be an ideal opportunity to find out what their strategies are.'

'Strategies, what soddin' strategies?'

'They must have a strategy to get a cup; they need one otherwise the ground goes back to the landlord – he wants it for building land. The good news is we could flit, no problem.'

Geoffrey looked up and smiled. 'Flit eh? We've a brand new one, just come out, you can tell me what you think?' He rummaged amongst other bottles in the back of the car. He held out two of them and flicked off the tops with his thumbs. As the froth poured onto the floor, he said, 'Go on then, how?'

'Simple,' said Albert, belching back the gas from the beer. 'All we have to do is stop these bastards from winning a cup.' He indicated the pitch, using the bottle as a pointer.

'You can't do that, it's unethical … illegal… You can't stop somebody winning … can you?'

'We have to do something so that I can retire and go back to being a happy man, not a miserable bastard like I am now.' Albert's eyes started to fill up. 'Jesus, now look at me. We have to do something.' He rooted for a hanky in his damp trousers.

Albert did not go out much these days and the nearest he came to drinking alcohol was sipping his wife's sloe gin in measured amounts. So as the effect of Old Goat's Horn kicked in, his voice got louder and his language stronger. Through a tear-soaked hanky, he ranted at Geoffrey. 'So you'd rather stay here forever, would you, being battered by bleedin' cricket balls and living in negative bleedin' equity? Well you've got three months to do something or it's another ten long soddin' years.'

Geoffrey leaned forward and put a hand over Albert's mouth, hushing him and looking round.

'Keep your voice down. OK, go on then,' he urged.

They huddled together but Albert had now lost the ability to speak and Geoffrey began to lose the will to listen. Shortly after, Geoffrey supported Albert with one arm round his waist while he rang the front doorbell. 'Sorry, Mrs Bradley, didn't mean this to happen,' he said as he helped Albert inside.

Later, Albert recounted to his wife how all of a sudden his legs would no longer support him and his tongue appeared to have doubled in size.

'See you've made a big hit with the neighbours,' said Susan when Geoffrey finally came to bed.

'Don't you start! You said you were just going to help out with the teas. Apparently, you're making a name for yourself as Little Miss Know-it-all.'

No other communication occurred that night; the only link between them was the stretched material of the duvet as they slept back to back.

New Day Dawns

The sun was shining and the birds were singing as Sir Alf whizzed down the country lane on the outskirts of the village. Being able to feel the wind in his face was a brand new sensation. 'Should have done this years ago,' he mused. 'But what's done is done.'

His new 'GT' chair, as he called it, had given him back some of the independence that he had enjoyed before the accident. Each time he went out, he ventured further and further afield. He had got used to the new chair's handling but as the novelty of the neck-snapping acceleration and tyre-screeching brakes wore off, he rarely used it to its full potential.

He was savouring the peace and solitude from a viewpoint overlooking the moors when he was interrupted by his other aid to autonomy. As he fumbled to get at his mobile phone hidden at the bottom of his panniers, he apologised to all within earshot. 'Sorry, sorry, it's under my sandwiches.'

They were not impressed. 'Come out for a bit of peace, what's he want to bring that thing for?' mumbled a rambler, his map case fluttering in the breeze. When Sir Alf answered in his usual loud voice, a group of picnickers packed up and moved on, letting him know their feelings on the subject of modern communications. 'Shouldn't be allowed, should be banned,' said an elderly but hardy lady, pulling her hood over her head.

'It's Terry Cargill here, can you hear me?'

'Yes, loud and clear.'

Another group of picnickers nodded in agreement. 'We can all bloody hear you!'

Sir Alf sensed their displeasure and whispered into the receiver. 'I'll get back to you in five minutes.' He pressed the off button and apologised again to the few people who remained.

Further down the lane, he dialled Terry Cargill's number by selecting the memory button. When he bought the phone, the instructions advised that up to fifty numbers could be stored on its memory. Up to now, he only had five which showed, he thought, how empty his existence had become.

'Is that you Alf? Reception's not so good,' said Terry, speaking slowly.

'What have you got for me?' asked Sir Alf.

'Well, it's like this. Apparently you signed over all the managerial responsibility to your Roland for the duration of your incapacity.'

'Meaning what?'

'I suppose it depends on your interpretation of the word "incapacity".'

'You mean that although I'm sound in my head, because I'm in a wheelchair I'm considered incapacitated?'

'Something like that. Have you had physio?' asked Terry, trying to be helpful.

'You need some feeling, some sensation, something for them to work with apparently,' Sir Alf replied, his voice beginning to taper off. 'Thanks anyway. I'll be in touch.'

He made his way back up the hill to the viewpoint, this time making sure the phone was switched off. He stared out across the hills; it had all the ingredients of a scenic landscape painting, but all he could see was bankruptcy and permanent disability.

A brightly dressed rambler nearby was pouring his similarly dressed wife a cup of steaming tea from a flask.

As they dunked their biscuits, she looked at Alf and smiled. 'Grand to be alive, isn't it,' she mused wistfully in a voice that carried.

He looked in their direction, and then set off home. He entered the front door to be confronted by Flora vacuuming the hall carpet. 'You still here?' he queried.

'I'll go now if you want.'

'Sorry, I've had a bad day,' he apologised. 'Fancy a coffee?'

'But you set off happy as Larry. What happened?'

'I've had a call from my solicitor. The bottom line is this: if I remain in this chair much longer, our Roland will bankrupt the lot of us.'

Flora poured hot water into the mugs and pondered. 'It seems strange to have your own son, who you see most mornings, in a position that he can ruin you. Have you tried talking to him? Surely he can see sense if…'

'It's like this: I made him the boss and now he thinks he knows best and rides roughshod over anybody who says different. I've tried talking to him from all angles, as a father, as a businessman, as a friend even. Just ends in a row. Then he says I should look after myself and let him get on with running the business. Well, we only agreed that he could run the show while I'm incapacitated, in other words, stuck in this frigging chair. The thing is, according to the doctors, I should be well on my way by now but nowt seems to be happening, no feeling … see.' As if to demonstrate, he slapped the top of his leg. 'Nothing.'

'You have to believe in what the doctors say. You might just have to wait a bit longer, that's all,' Flora said unconvincingly.

'In the meantime, the mill goes down the pan,' Sir Alf said more abruptly than he intended. 'And now Miriam's buggered off. Found a note on the side this morning, no details, just buggered off.'

They drank the coffee in silence, both busy with their own thoughts.

Susan Has Her Say

Arthur Padstow read out the minutes of the last meeting and asked for a seconder. Without hesitation or consideration, Tom Deakin raised his hand, then went back to his conversation with Fred Pickup about it being the longest day and how from now on the nights would start to draw in.

Susan raised her hand, 'Point of order Mr Chairman.' The conversation stopped and everyone looked up. 'The minutes are a legally binding document and proper regard should be given to them. The impression I get is that they're only being given cursory consideration.'

'What are you suggesting?' barked Tom.

'All I'm saying is that when you seconded those minutes, you hardly looked up from your chat.'

Tom immediately stood up, threw the agenda across the table, and announced, 'I don't have to put up with this crap! I resign! Get yourselves another groundsman! Shove that in your bleeding agenda.'

The rest of them, including Susan, looked aghast as he slammed the door behind him. John Appleby's plea of, 'Tom, Tom, oh Tom,' went unheard.

Janice turned on him. 'This is your fault, you've as much idea about running a meeting as I don't know what. If you'd kept a tighter rein in the past, this wouldn't have happened.'

Arthur, now inflamed, chipped in. 'Excuse me, are you saying that we don't take these meetings seriously? That's an insult after all the unpaid hours I've put in. Let's see how you manage on your own then.' He, too, threw the agenda on the table and left.

'This is all down to you,' Janice said, pointing at John. Then, as her eyes filled with tears, 'Look what you've done now.'

She got out a tissue and wiped her eyes, smearing mascara across her face. She looked at the blackened tissue, then in the tiny mirror in her handbag. 'I can't stay, not like this.' She duly grabbed her coat and left.

Fred and John stared at Susan. 'Happy now?' said Fred.

Susan stared at the table.

'No point continuing, we're not quorate. Think I'll grab a pint where there's less aggro,' said John wearily.

'I'm sorry, I just thought that...'

'Don't worry love, they'll come back. Seen it all before' said John, putting on his coat.

'After you've apologised, that is,' said Fred icily.

'Take no notice. There's been a bit of pressure this year. Folk are a bit on edge. This Roland Bullock business is getting on us nerves,' said John, trying to ease her feelings.

As Susan entered the hallway Geoffrey, not taking his eyes from the TV, unknowingly rubbed salt into the wound. 'You're home early, did you sack them all?'

Susan ignored the comment and went straight into the kitchen. She flicked the top off one of his free samples and drank from the bottle.

Flora Does Some Research

Flora had spread the library books out on the kitchen table and was leafing through the pages. She loved the aroma of the ink as she opened each page. She was grateful to Sir Alf; it was he who had employed her in the first place. The job was relaxed and easy-going and she enjoyed the banter, so she was determined to help him get over the problem of his legs. She flipped open a page at random; it opened on a picture of massage techniques applied to a scantily clad lady.

'If it's stimulation you want!' she grinned, then cocked an ear as she heard her mother's footsteps coming down the hall. She shut the book with a bang as her mother entered the kitchen and scanned the array of books. The look on her mother's face indicated she was not pleased.

She was used to her daughter's unpredictable ways. 'What you up to now?' she said impatiently.

'Oh, hello Flora, have you had a nice day?' Flora retaliated. They were getting off to yet another bad start.

'What's this, another fad? Like being a vegetarian, then craving bacon sandwiches. Or condemning the French, but eating their apples.' As she spotted the titles of her daughter's latest obsession, she was almost lost for words. She opened a well-thumbed page to reveal a naked couple in the process of reciprocal manipulation. '*Aromatherapy for Beginners, Full Body Massage Techniques*? Don't let your dad see these, he'll go bloody mad. What do you want these for, anyway?'

'Because I'm interested in it, OK?' Flora slammed the heavy book shut. 'Look, they do this at night school. It can't be iffy if they do it at night school.' She gathered the books and marched towards the door. 'Whatever I'm interested in, you've got a problem with it.'

Flora's mum had been here before. 'Piggy in the middle again,' she thought as Flora went on. Then she heard herself repeating similar lines to the ones she always used: 'He only wants what's best for you. He doesn't want you getting into trouble. If he sees books like these, he'll get the wrong idea!'

Flora thumped up the stairs and slammed her bedroom door.

Her mother stared at the kettle that seemed to be refusing to boil and mused, 'I'm defending the soddin' bigot and he's not even here. I never used to be like this.' She sniffed back a tear as the kettle's whistle got louder. She blew her nose on a piece of floral kitchen towel and then reached for the comfort of the biscuit barrel.

Susan Applies Some Pressure

Susan approached the reception desk in Joseph Lagg Estate Agents. She had already looked at the boards containing details of properties in the area, particularly the ones on the border of the cricket pitch.

'This has been here a while,' she said, pointing at one to see the reaction.

Julia, the secretary looked up and gave a rehearsed response. 'Not much moving but things aren't as bad as last year. Would you like to see inside?'

'Not now, thanks. I've just popped in to see Mr Lagg.'

'He's busy with a client, but shouldn't be much longer … been in an hour now.'

It was then that Susan spotted the personal number plate on the new Jaguar outside the shop. 'RB1, posh car,' she pried.

'Yes, it's Mr Bullock's. All right, isn't it?'

'Roland Bullock?'

'Yes, colleague of Mr Lagg.'

Susan made herself comfortable in the little waiting area.

'You'll wait then?' enquired Julia.

Susan looked up from the *Horse and Hound* magazine provided to lift the tone. 'Oh yes,' she replied crisply.

Julia pressed down the button on the antique communication system. 'Sorry to disturb you Mr Lagg, but there's a Mrs Perkins waiting to see you.'

Joe Lagg dreaded that name, and in a panic held down the speak button by mistake. 'Shit! Tell her I'll be out soon.'

Two customers who had just entered the office turned around and left while Susan grinned behind the magazine.

'I think Mrs Perkins got the message, Mr Lagg,' Julia sighed.

On the other side of the party wall, Roland was preparing to leave. 'Ah … this is the lady who puts the fear of God into you. Better not keep *her* waiting then.'

In the reception area, Roland and Susan caught each other's eye then quickly looked away, neither wanting to give away any clues.

Joe stood in the doorway of his office, watching as Roland climbed into his car. 'Come in Mrs Perkins, always good to see you. Coffee?'

Susan spoke plainly. 'Come across the word "hypocrite" in your crossword recently?'

'What's that supposed to mean?'

'Good to see you Mrs Perkins,' mimicked Susan.

'All right, all right, it's just that the market's a bit slow and you want your problem solving right now. It might take a bit longer than we thought,' he said, unable to look her in the face.

'Bullshit!' snapped Susan angrily. 'You've done nothing to sort this out. You ripped us off at the start and now you're just stalling.'

Joe pushed a coffee cup and a plate of biscuits towards her. 'That's not true; things are happening. I know it's not obvious, but things *are* happening behind the scenes.'

'OK, tell me what you're doing then.'

'I can't, it'd be betraying a confidence, but you have my word that it'll be sorted.'

Susan sipped her coffee. 'Your word? How can I trust someone who swindles you in the first place, then won't explain how he plans to sort it?'

'Just trust me, OK.'

'How long before things happen?'

'Couple of weeks, maybe three.'

Susan picked up a Bourbon from the plate. 'Dubious friends you've got,' she said through a mouthful of crumbs.

'That wasn't a friend, it was a colleague, and that's my business!' he snapped defensively.

'Touchy! But how did you know I was referring to Roland Bullock? See you in a fortnight.' Susan sneered at him and strutted out.

As Julia cleared the cups, she smiled mischievously. She leaned over Joe's shoulder then half-whispered, 'Just how much does she know?'

An Apologetic Albert Bradley

Albert Bradley gently rapped the knocker of the Perkins' household. He had been working himself up to the visit for a couple of days and had been practising his apology most of the afternoon.

'I'll get it!' shouted Geoffrey.

As the door opened, Albert tried to smile but failed. He could not remember ever having apologised to anyone before. He certainly had not smiled properly for years, so the next few minutes were going to be a bit of a challenge.

'I've come about the other night, don't know what came over me.' The words felt like broken glass in his throat.

'Not a problem,' replied Geoffrey.

'I'd have come sooner, but I've been ill for days, couldn't stop shaking, retching all the first night then dizzy spells. Bleedin' awful taste and gas… Jesus, banished to the garden at one point.' Albert held his head and his backside as he explained.

'Some hangover, eh? Fancy a drink?' Geoffrey laughed, exhibiting zero sympathy. 'That Old Goat's Horn, what a cracker!'

'You're very kind, but tea will do nicely,' said Albert holding his stomach as though he could feel rumblings.

They sat at the kitchen table and drank milky tea, though Albert spilled most of his as he still had not got rid of the shakes. 'Sorry,' he apologised, as the tea formed a puddle round his cup.

'Never mind that. This business with the cricket club, run it by me again,' said Geoffrey, wiping the table.

Albert looked up. 'In a nutshell, the club has to win a cup. If they can't, the ground goes back to the Bullocks, they build houses on it and we get the going rate for ours.'

'Seems a bit much to have our house prices resting on whether a team wins or not.'

'Precisely,' said Albert.

'But you can't help the other teams win, can you?' queried Geoffrey.

'No, but maybe you can prevent Throttle from winning.' Albert's face changed to a sinister leer. 'It's like this: we have to ensure that at vital stages of certain matches things happen that prevent play continuing. Or, we could see to it that vital players aren't fit, or are called away, or sommat.' Albert's leer turned to a beaming smile.

'Sounds decidedly dodgy if you ask me, especially if someone not a million miles away finds out.'

Geoffrey nodded towards the living room. Susan, engrossed in a televised 'whodunnit', was unaware of the shenanigans being plotted in her own kitchen. 'If she ever finds out, we are deceased, and I mean stone cold, on the slab deceased.' Geoffrey mimicked the expression of a person being hanged.

'But if it's half the market price of your house or their cup, what's it to be?'

Teacups clashed across the kitchen table as they toasted their new alliance. 'Cobblers to the cricket,' they harmonised in hushed tones. Their expressions turned to horror when they heard Susan's voice.

'Not sure if I approve of grown men whispering in kitchens. You'll be wearing funny outfits next.'

'Not up to anything,' said Geoffrey.

'I didn't say you were. Sounds like somebody has got a guilty conscience. How's your head Albert? I believe you've been ill. Stopped farting, have you? Something in Old Goat's Horn, Geoffrey does nothing else.' She did not wait for a reply, just smirked, grabbed the biscuit box and returned to watch the second part of her film.

They sat motionless in the kitchen, and then Geoffrey nodded towards the back door. Once outside, he gently closed it.

'What do you reckon?' asked Albert, thumbing towards the closed door.

Geoffrey shrugged his shoulders. 'Not a clue any more, mate,' he sighed.

Rest and Recuperation

The following Saturday, Geoffrey arrived home after plying his ale samples. Based on his reasonable success, he decided to test his product for quality and performance. Recently he had wallowed in the delights of being a couch potato. The few hours of doing 'what the hell I like' while Susan and Alison were at the cricket had become a refuge from the mayhem of work and, he was sorry to say, the bedlam of home.

He was not a keen football supporter, but he enjoyed a game with lots of action. If there was a good film on the other channel, he would flick between the two to double the entertainment. He had tried to develop the skill of flicking between three stations but this taxed his limited concentration. On more than one occasion, he had been found fast asleep, bottle and remote control still gripped firmly in his hands.

He had settled down to a second-rate film and athletics, neither of which could overcome the soporific effect of the beer, when he was rudely plucked from his semi-slumber. Although it was only Susan and Alison returning early, to Geoffrey it sounded like a cross between an angry mob and a herd of cattle charging down the hallway.

'What the hell's going on?' he remarked as they flew straight past him and entered the kitchen.

'They could have killed him, killed all of them for that matter,' wailed Susan.

Peeved as he was at the intrusion, he thought it sensible to enquire about the apparent attempted murder. 'Killed who?' he said, poking his head round the kitchen door.

'Ben, Ben... for goodness' sake, who else?' yelled Susan.

Geoffrey looked at Alison and mouthed, 'Who's Ben?'

Alison, taking after her mother, was also devoid of patience. 'Daddy, don't you know anything? It's Benjamin … Benjamin's been hurt.'

Geoffrey had been harbouring unpleasant suspicions about Benjamin and consequently cared little for his welfare. So, as his sincerity faded, he could only offer a crass comment. 'Slip on the grass, did he?'

They looked daggers at him. Susan pulled Alison towards her, put her hands over her ears and hissed, 'You bastard, they could have died. Didn't you see the ambulance?'

Geoffrey's brain raced. 'Beginning to lose this one,' he thought. He had learned to think quickly in situations like this, situations that unfortunately were becoming more common. He immediately decided against stating the real reason: 'I didn't see the ambulance or its flashing blue light because I was horizontal in an alcoholic stupor' and went for the 'feigning compassion' routine.

Holding out his palms and employing a pained expression, he said, 'So what on earth's happened?'

'Someone tried to kill the team!' shouted Alison, basking in the hysteria.

Geoffrey, still not convinced and unable to resist putting his foot in it, added, 'Aren't we exaggerating a bit here? After all, I haven't heard any bombs going off.' He looked at their dumbstruck faces and offered a watery smile.

'They were poisoned, you idiot!' said Susan.

Geoffrey screwed up his face in disbelief. 'On a cricket pitch? How?'

'They came out after tea, and within minutes some of them couldn't see. Benjamin was holding his throat because he couldn't breathe. The match had to be abandoned.'

'So who made the tea then?' he asked hesitantly.

'Me and three other ladies and we've already had this enquiry. If it'd been the food, both teams would've gone down and most of the spectators. As it happens, only half our team was affected. Someone poisoned them.' There was a moment's silence and then Susan asked the question that Geoffrey was dying to pose. 'Who'd want to poison our own team?'

'Can't think. Was it an important game?' he asked tentatively, an excited tremor creeping into his voice.

Alison gave him the answer he was waiting for: 'They were playing the top of the league.'

'So what happens to the points? Do they split them? Are they lost or do they have to play again?' asked Geoffrey. He then realised he had overstepped the mark.

Susan stared at him in disbelief. 'Have you no feelings? People are nearly killed and all you can ask about is the points! Get your coat, Alison.'

'Where are you going?' he asked.

'We're going visiting; he's being kept in for observation.'

As the door slammed, Geoffrey grabbed another bottle, settled down on the sofa and pondered. 'Well done, Albert. I don't know how you did it but well done.'

The Day After the Poisoning

At the Ram Inn, normal Sunday discussions gave way to the events of the previous day.

'Bastards should be hung,' remarked a local.

'Hanging's too good; they should be burnt at the stake with their entrails hanging…'

People moved away from the individual with sadistic inclinations.

At the rear of the pub, Roland, Joe and the Jakeson brothers sipped their beer in quiet reflection.

'You could have killed them, you stupid bastard. If they find out, we're on porridge,' hissed Joe.

'Keep your voice down, there's a lynch mob over there,' Roland mumbled. He tried not to stare at the rough, unshaven individual at the bar who, in his mind, would have no problem stringing those responsible for the poisoning from the rafters, then would continue with his drinking.

Feeling aggrieved at the lack of appreciation for a job well done, Reginald Jakeson made no apologies. 'You said hinder play, prevent them winning.'

Joe, who was getting angrier by the minute and could have sworn he could taste porridge, replied, 'Hinder play, we said. Prevent them winning, we also said. We did not say kill them!'

Simon, who, as the years advanced was becoming more and more like the character in the nursery rhyme, offered a comment. 'How was we to know he'd lick the ball?'

Roland and Joe stared then, in unison, they urged, 'Go on.'

'Reginald kept the umpire talking while I stole the ball out of his pocket. It were right easy,' explained Simon.

'They keep hold of it during tea to prevent tampering, ironic like,' added Reginald.

'I painted it, put it under the drier in the gents, and then put it back.'

Roland looked puzzled. 'Let me get this right, you painted it. What with, emulsion?'

'No, it were a mixture of black cap mushrooms, nettle and laburnum leaves, put in a blender, whizzed, then sieved. It's the clear liquid that's painted on,' Reginald explained.

'Where'd you get this from, a frigging witch doctor?' Roland spat out in exasperation.

'No, our mum uses it.'

'Your mum uses it! What for? Getting rid of the neighbours? Euthanasia?'

Simon looked at Reginald. 'Euthy what?'

'Killing old folk,' he clarified.

Reginald turned to the others. 'She puts it on the fence to keep the cats out.'

'And does it?' asked Joe.

'Oh yes, they never come back,' he smiled.

Joe held his head in his hands. 'That's because they're all dead; they don't come back because they're dead. Jesus, what have I got mixed up with here?'

'It were only supposed to make 'em itch and their eyes water, only the pro went and licked the ball... Game *were* abandoned though, we got a result,' said Reginald positively.

'That's because there weren't enough players left to play,' Joe said, head still in hands.

'You were lucky this time. We just want you to be more careful, that's all. Basically we're pleased with what you've done but you have to be more subtle,' Roland said. He got up and left without finishing his beer.

Joe felt the need for anaesthetic from the day's events and ordered another pint. He left Reginald explaining the word 'subtle' to Simon. 'It's how mothers feed their babies, but I haven't sussed the connection yet. Strange bloke, that Roland.'

Joe, beginning to despair, turned to watch the big match on the widescreen that had been reinstated to lure back the locals.

***

Later that afternoon, Albert was washing his car in the drive. Stooping to rinse the sponge, he got the feeling he was being watched. Looking to one side, he noticed Geoffrey standing at the living-room window. Immediately they made eye contact, Geoffrey started winking and making exaggerated thumbs-up gestures. Albert, unaware of what he was getting at, shrugged his shoulders.

Minutes later, Geoffrey was standing at the fence. 'Well done, Albert,' he said excitedly in a low voice.

'Well done what?' Albert was grumpy at being disturbed from another task he had come to detest.

'It was you, wasn't it?'

'What was me?'

'It was you who poisoned the team and got the game called off.'

'What do you think I am, an effing serial killer? Do you think I'd poison the whole team just to get the match stopped?' Albert waved a dripping sponge. 'You must have a poor impression of me if you think I'd do a thing like that.' He walked towards the tap in the garage.

Geoffrey's head dropped. 'Sorry, Albert, I should have known better.'

Albert turned off the tap while Geoffrey, standing in the garage doorway, scratched his head in a vain attempt to get his brains cells working. 'So who … who would kill the whole team to stop the game?' he wondered aloud. He looked up to see Albert with that fiendish expression on his face, the same as the other night in the kitchen.

'It doesn't follow that whoever did it wanted to kill the whole team. Maybe they only wanted to kill one person but as a cover-up, they were prepared to kill them all.'

Geoffrey, not convinced but not wanting to hurt his feelings, tempered his comment. 'Seems a trifle extreme! So who?'

'Could be anyone. Could be any husband wanting to get even with the pro,' smirked Albert. Then, imitating a fishwife, he beckoned Geoffrey over. 'I've heard that wherever the pro plays, he has it away with any number of women and there's a horde of angry husbands just waiting for the right moment. You never know, it could be a bloke from round here. Apparently he's had his share of this village already.'

Geoffrey stared at him glumly. He mused over Albert's comments for the rest of the day, his mind veering from one scene to the next. Susan's apparent over-familiarity, the episode where the pro had carried her into the house, her mood swings and lack of affection. In Geoffrey's mind, it all added up to the unthinkable. 'Keep calm. Get to the bottom of it but don't put your foot in it.' The mixed metaphors made him smile. He had not felt much like smiling recently, what with one thing and another.

'Jesus!' he shouted in frustration, his voice echoing in the empty house.

Susan and Alison had gone back to the hospital, and he began to regret the offhand comment he had thrown down the hallway as they left. 'Off to visit the sick, are you?' the words tripping uncontrollably from his tongue.

Recently he had started to think aloud and offer his problems to inanimate objects. It helped in some ways to get the problem out in the open, but answers were a rarity. He stood in front of the hall mirror and pleaded his case.

'All this pressure of a new job, a new house and deadlines to keep. No support, no cuddles, no amour.' He paused, grabbed imaginary lapels and gesticulated as if in a courtroom. 'I'm a simple man with simple needs. I drink a bit and it's been made clear this is frowned upon. I don't smoke. So how is a man supposed to get rid of his tension other than beer or amour? And I'm not getting my share!' he bellowed. 'I rest my case.'

Then a movement caught his eye. He turned to the front door and observed the distorted facial features of his wife and daughter as they pressed against the frosted glass. Holding open the front door, he asked, 'How is he then?'

From the kitchen, Susan replied, 'Better than you, from what I've just seen!'

The Brewery

Anthony Dawes and Geoffrey Perkins were having a progress meeting at the Old Goat Brewery. They sat opposite one another. As Geoffrey recounted to his wife each Monday evening, 'progress' related to 'How much have you sold?'

Anthony Dawes opened proceedings: 'So what's the verdict? Are the targets achievable?'

A simple 'no' would have been the correct answer but Geoffrey, not wanting to appear defeatist, used his usual logic in this all-too-familiar situation and lied. 'Of course they are, just got to get round a few more clubs. Once they try out the freebies, they're hooked.'

'What's the general feeling about the new brew?'

'There's no doubting the punters like the taste. It's just that it's so strong they can't remember what they've had,' Geoffrey advised, leaning back on his chair.

'Always been a problem with strong ale. Never mind, you seem to be shifting 'em OK, but we haven't had many large orders yet.'

In reality, most clubs were afraid to have the strong brew on the premises. 'We'd love to, but they start knocking lumps out of one another. We heard what happened at Throttle,' was the usual reply to his sales patter.

Geoffrey was in fact drinking most of the freebies himself, so it was a curious but timely moment when fate took the shape of the local police officer and a man from the Environmental Health Department.

'Sorry to interrupt, can we have a word?' The police officer's massive frame dwarfed the doorway. He ducked down to avoid the top of the doorframe with his helmet.

'Course you can. What's up?' stuttered Anthony.

'We're investigating the incident at the cricket club.' The officer's voice sounded even more formal.

'Why, what's happened?' Anthony turned to Geoffrey. 'Do you know anything about this?'

Geoffrey opened his mouth to speak, but was cut off by the man from the council. 'We're here to investigate the alleged poisoning of several members of the Throttle Cricket Club team, particularly one Mr Benjamin Winston who required hospitalisation.'

'Hospitalisation?' repeated Anthony.

'Witnesses have stated that Mr Winston drank at least two bottles of beer, supplied by you, prior to going back on the pitch. He subsequently fell ill with a throat condition from which he nearly died.'

Anthony and Geoffrey stared at one another. Then Anthony let loose. 'Are you saying that our ale poisoned him?'

'We're not saying anything at the moment, other than we are investigating the incident. Therefore anything he consumed prior to becoming ill is under enquiry,' added the man officiously.

'We've sold hundreds of bottles and no complaints… Isn't that right, Geoffrey?' Anthony said.

They all looked at Geoffrey. His mind raced for an answer. This would be the second occasion within minutes where he pondered the consequences of telling the truth. He hesitated no longer. 'Hundreds! Not one complaint.'

'That's very good to hear. But until your beer gets the all clear, we are putting a prohibition order on it. In other words, you are not allowed to sell any more. We'll also need a sample from the same batch.'

Anthony, shocked, rose from his chair. 'And you'll help us with the overdraft, go see the bank manager about the cash flow, will you? This is a business we're trying to run here, not a frigging Mickey Mouse shop. We can't afford to stop production just like that.'

The officer nodded to the man from the council, then spoke. 'Don't make this more difficult than it already is, sir. If you could let us have the samples, we'll be on our way. The quicker we get them tested, the sooner you get back in production...'

'How long?' Anthony sighed.

'A day or two at most.'

Anthony slumped back in his chair. 'Sort them out will you, Geoffrey.'

Geoffrey smiled and led them out. 'This way, gents. Fancy a pint before you go? We've got a new brew just finished clearing, absolutely gorgeous it is.'

That evening, after Susan had listened to Geoffrey's account of the day, she received a call from John Appleby. 'I wonder if you could attend an emergency meeting?' he said, sounding like a man suffering from sleep deprivation.

'Well, yes,' she replied, surprised to be asked back. 'But won't you be a bit short-handed after all the resignations?'

'No, not really, everyone will be there.'

'So have they all taken back their notices to quit?'

'Well, yes and no...' he dithered. 'Actually, I phoned them all up and asked them to come back, pleaded really. I had to and they all agreed.'

'What, just like that?' she said with disbelief.

'Well, not just like that.' He paused and took in a breath of air. 'I promised them that you'd apologise. We'd have gone belly up. No groundsman, no treasurer, no tea lady. I had no choice. I'm sorry, I really am.'

'You're sorry! Sounds like it's going to be me that's sorry. So what've you told them?' she said, more amused than annoyed.

'All I've said is that you're sorry you overreacted, that's all. Anyway, the meeting's at half seven.'

'I'll be there, but don't expect sackcloth and ashes.' She held the receiver as it clicked and went dead. 'Bastard,' she muttered.

An Extraordinary Meeting

The mood was somewhat chilly as the committee members took to their seats. John opened the proceedings. 'I'm sorry to do this to you on a free night but as you can appreciate, these are extenuating circumstances.'

He took off his glasses, rubbed his face and then, with an audible sigh, continued. 'I'd also like to say that at the previous meeting I think feelings and tensions were running high. If we can all agree to let bygones be bygones, we can get down to the proper business of finding out what the hell happened last Saturday.'

Ever since the phone call, Susan had been thinking about what she might say at the meeting. She intended to call them all 'spineless bastards who couldn't run a piss-up in a brewery' before tipping over the table and walking out giving them the V sign. In the end, she did what she had to do in order to maintain contact with Benjamin. She consoled herself that half an hour in the hut with Benjamin more than compensated for putting up with these moaning bastards once a month.

Through gritted teeth, she purposefully addressed the chairman without making eye contact with the others. 'I'd just like to say, Mr Chairman, that I apologise to all concerned for any offence caused by my overreaction at the last meeting.'

The others, grateful to hear the remorse, thawed out.

'Aye lass, we all regret what happened,' said Tom Deakin. He smiled and stood up, 'Mind if I have a pint? It's thirsty work this apologising. Anyone else?'

Having broken the ice, everyone returned to the table with full glasses. John resumed the meeting. 'Things have taken on a great pace today, what with the police and everything. Bottom line is they've interviewed Janice and the ladies who helped at the match. They have been given the all clear. Bloody common sense to me, everyone ate the same. They've checked the supplier of the meat and the temperature of our fridge and it's OK.' He looked round for responses but none came. 'Next item then. I'll be as tactful as I can, so bear with me.' He looked straight at Susan: 'Susan,' he said pointedly.

Susan, who had started to drift away from the proceedings, sat up with a start. Her mind raced: she'd been spotted coming out of the shed, Benjamin had said something, broken marriage, scandal, divorce… Perspiration formed on her forehead.

'What?' she snapped.

Taken aback by the volume of her reply, John added, 'Don't take it personal.'

Susan butted in. 'For God's sake, what?'

'The beer he drank, it was your Geoffrey's.'

'Oh, that,' she said. She had been readying herself to own up to the affair and tell them not to poke their noses into her business. 'Jesus!' she sighed.

'I know it's bad news for Geoffrey,' John apologised. 'But we have no option but to ban it till the source of the poisoning is found.'

'Point of order Mr Chairman, point of order,' Tom Deakin interrupted. 'I must protest at this miscarriage of justice here.'

Janice turned to the chairman, screwed up her face in disbelief and mouthed silently, 'Miscarriage of justice?'

Tom, sensing his supply of freebies was about to dry up, offered himself as a witness for the defence. 'Your Geoffrey supplied the beer that morning, a six pack for the pro and another to be put behind the bar for emergencies. The pro has consumed his allocation, I've consumed most of the emergency stock.' The others smiled at his confession. 'Other than the usual, there have been no adverse effects so I think you'll have to look elsewhere for your culprit.'

'There were more than the pro affected,' butted in Fred. 'Albeit only mildly.'

'You're right. I think the police will have to look elsewhere for the poisoner. Meanwhile, we can't sell it or even give it away. Any remaining stock will have to be quarantined.'

He smirked mischievously and gazed at Tom who, in turn, stared at the remaining three bottles on the bar.

'Next item, we're only seven games away from the end of the season. We're fifth in the league and still in the run for the cup but with Ben temporarily out of the frame, we might have to get another pro. I'm afraid Bullock's axe still hangs over us.'

A Quiet Breakfast?

Sir Alf and Roland were having breakfast. They had moved on from continuous rowing to eating in total silence. Neither wanted to be in the other's company for long and so what used to be a relaxed three-quarters of an hour was now a hasty munch of toast, a gulp of coffee and through the door. On this occasion, Sir Alf was leafing through the mid-week version of *The Throttle Flyer*. He read out the headline with disbelief: *Big Ben Struck – Poisoner Sought*.

'Don't pull any punches, this editor.' Then he read out the details. 'Attempted murder, perhaps by someone who harbours a grudge. What the hell is this world coming to?'

Thinking there had been a major incident that he was unaware of, Roland pricked up his ears.

'Someone's tried to poison the whole bloody cricket team. Good Jesus, mass murder right here in Throttle!' Sir Alf said, forgetting his resolve never to speak in Roland's presence.

On hearing this, the coffee Roland was about to swallow took a detour and went down the wrong way. Moments later, it came back through his nose. He grabbed a napkin and held it to his face as he found himself convulsing and losing control. Sir Alf looked over the top of his paper as his son tried to regain his composure. Roland excused himself from the table and left with tears of coffee rolling down his cheeks.

Sir Alf had started to read the article again when Flora entered. 'Has Master Roland finished?' she said, looking down at the mess on the table.

'Let's just say he couldn't keep it down,' he replied, not taking his eyes off the article. 'Have you heard about the poisoning?' He was fully aware that she was the fount of all knowledge when it came to sordid goings-on in the village.

'Shocking business, pro nearly died and the others nearly blinded. They still don't know what caused it. There's talk about revenge, you know, somebody had it in for the pro.'

He looked at her and squinted. 'Really? All this going on in a poky place like this?'

'It has to happen somewhere, so it might as well be here,' she suggested.

Roland, now recovered and in a clean shirt, was eavesdropping at the breakfast-room door. 'Great,' he quietly applauded, 'Revenge motive … why didn't *I* think of that?'

Flora and Sir Alf turned their heads sharply as they heard the front door slam shut.

'Strange one, that,' Alf said with a sigh of disappointment. Flora thought it best not to ask, so she just nodded as she cleaned the table. 'Funny things, kids. I thought I did all the right things for him and look how he's turned out. Got to the point where we hardly speak.'

Flora nodded again.

'The way he reacted, you'd think he had something to do with it.'

'Never!' Flora said, folding the coffee-stained tablecloth.

'Crikey! Fancy thinking my own son could do a thing like that!'

'Roland wouldn't dream of it,' added Flora, trying to disguise her true thoughts. 'Come on, it's a brilliant day. Fancy a walk?' She glanced through the window, and then realised what she had just said. 'You know what I mean. I'll come with you, if you like,' she added sheepishly, looking at the floor.

'Aye, let's get some fresh air. I'll see you in the hallway.'

A stiff breeze aided them as they crunched down the drive. Then, turning sharp right away from the village, the wind blew in their faces and brought tears to their eyes.

'This'll get rid of the cobwebs,' said Sir Alf, searching in his pocket for his hanky.

Flora walked alongside. 'Alf, can I say something?'

'I know what you're going to say but spit it out anyway,' he said, staring straight ahead.

'It's just that recently you've become distant. We used to have fun,' she said.

'It's nowt to do with you, Flora. It's just that I woke up the other day and felt so miserable, right through to my marrow. Haven't been able to shake it off. Since I've been getting out in this chair, it's revived memories of what it was like before. I used to be so active, and on top of that...' He paused to choose his words carefully: 'I've a feeling that our Roland is up to no good. I haven't got to the bottom of it yet, but I'm getting closer. Point is ... if I'm right ... what then?'

'For a minute I thought you'd gone off me,' said Flora with relief.

They arrived at the viewpoint at the top of the hill, and then faced the vista of the rolling hills above the village.

'We haven't played our game for ages. Don't you think about me any more?' she probed.

Again, he paused and thought carefully. 'It's not that I don't think about you. It's just that I wouldn't know what to do if, you know, the occasion arose.'

She knelt, gripped his leg and looked him in the eye: 'You just leave all that to me. Fancy a brew?'

They held on to the plastic cups of hot tea supplied by the vendor in the lay-by. As they surveyed the view, Sir Alf's eyes began to fill but not through the chill of the breeze.

Contemplation at Bullock Units

Roland sat in his swivel chair and pondered his next move. The Jakeson brothers' antics had scared him: a cold sweat had enveloped him when he found out about the poisoning. Since then, his imagination had run riot with alibis and explanations. He had the words in his mind like the script of a play, how he would disown the plot, and he would not hesitate from framing Joe and the Jakesons.

Seconds later, the voice of his secretary invaded his thoughts. 'Mr Bullock, a call for you.'

He picked up the receiver.

It was Joe; there was a nervous tremor in his voice. 'We need to talk,' he said.

'How about a pie and a pint?' Roland responded, pretending not to notice his distress.

They met in the pub, ordered a meal and sat in silence. Roland, unable to stand it any longer, broke the ice. 'They think it was revenge. They'll never suspect us of having anything to do with the poisoning. Couldn't have been better if we'd planned it ourselves.'

Unfortunately, Joe did not see it this way. 'Poisoning! I don't remember agreeing to poisoning!'

They both looked round to see if anyone had heard.

'Me neither, but we appear to have got away with it,' Roland replied smugly.

Joe, not convinced, carried on. 'I can't sleep proper for thinking what might have happened. I keep seeing myself in nick, explaining that we only meant to stop the game but ended up wiping out the whole soddin' team.'

'For God's sake calm down,' said Roland, getting concerned that Joe would give the game away.

The meal arrived and Roland tucked in. Joe picked up the knife and fork and stared at the utensils as they danced in his hands. They clattered on the table as he lost control.

'Get a grip,' Roland spluttered through a mouthful of pie and chips.

Joe picked at his meal. Then, unable to continue, he rested the knife and fork across his plate. It was an unfortunate choice of words from the waitress that set him off again. 'Is everything all right?' she said innocently.

'No, everything is not bloody well all right!' he barked.

Roland intervened: 'Sorry, love, the food's fine. Don't bother about my friend here, he's just had a bad day.'

The waitress scurried away carrying the used dishes. Minutes later, she returned nervously clutching a mini spiral-bound pad and a stubby pencil. 'Would you like dessert?' she croaked.

A remorseful Joe thanked her for asking but opted for the solace of the bar's top shelf. It was at this point that Roland started having doubts about their partnership. He began to view Joe as more of a puppet, someone to be used and manipulated, someone to do his dirty business. 'Let me get you another,' he said, viewing the gesture as an investment.

After two more off the top shelf, Joe became more relaxed. 'Pliable,' Roland thought. 'Now what are we going to do about this weekend's fixture?' he quizzed.

'Better ask the Jakesons, they seem to have it all in hand.' Joe downed his tot in one and grimaced as the rough alcohol bit the back of his throat.

Roland's tone changed to restrained irritation. 'They're your men, you engaged them. You find out what they've got planned.' He turned to the chap behind the bar. 'Bill, please.' He turned back to Joe. 'I'll give you a ring tomorrow. Have some answers.' Then he leaned closer and whispered with a hint of menace, 'Bit of advice, don't get pissed and mouth off!'

Joe nodded without making eye contact.

The afternoon wore on and the pub had filled up considerably by the time Joe left. As he stepped off his bar stool, he had to keep hold of the bar rail. He eyed the doorway and set off. 'A fortuitous circumstance,' he thought as he used the other customers for support as he made his way out.

The cool fresh air hit him in the face; he only just made it into the car park before he retched up the consumption of the past two hours. He staggered to the shop where his secretary helped him into his office and sat him in his chair.

'What on earth…?' She was about to ask what he had been up to but the stench of his breath put her in the picture. 'Ha, ha, self-inflicted, and this early in the week. Well, you'll get no sympathy from me,' she said.

Not wanting to listen to a lady half his age talk to him as if she was his mother, he retaliated. 'Just get me coffee and pills, or piss off and don't come back.'

Half an hour later, he ventured out to see where the coffee was. His day was complete when he cast his glazed eyes around the office. No coffee, no secretary or her belongings, just a manila envelope on her chair addressed to him. He did not open it. Instead, he turned the door sign to *Closed* and locked it. Returning to his office, he muttered, 'Shit, shit, shit.'

Hard Work Rewarded at *The Flyer*

'The shareholders would like to show their appreciation of your endeavours in raising sales by ten per cent. They're all very pleased,' said the regional manager as he held out an envelope.

Arnold Bosworth showed no restraint as he eagerly ripped it open. 'Thank you,' he beamed as he waved the cheque for five hundred pounds.

'Keep this up and there'll be another next month,' added the manager.

No Reward for Geoffrey

Geoffrey arrived home after a notably unsuccessful day to find the house empty. He had hoped for loving care and sympathy but his heart sank as he entered the hallway. 'Just great! Not a soul, no welcome home for the breadwinner, no food, no sod all! Well, bugger this.'

He dumped his briefcase in the hall and banged the front door behind him. As he marched down the drive, he heard someone whisper his name. 'Psst, Geoffrey, over here.'

Geoffrey turned to see Albert lurking in the corner of his garage. 'Come here,' he beckoned, crooking his finger.

Geoffrey's rumbling stomach always dominated his mood, and he was just about to die of hunger. 'A bit over the top, this. What the hell's up?' he said as they stood in the gloom of the unlit garage.

'It's about the game on Sunday. It's a cup match. Are you still on?'

'Still on what?'

'Don't mess me about, you know what I'm on about,' replied Albert.

'Yes, all right, so long as we don't kill anyone,' said Geoffrey.

'Now look, we've got to make sure the other side wins, though just at this moment I'm not sure how,' puzzled Albert.

'Simple, bribe the umpire.'

Albert smiled. 'Knew I could rely on you,' and then added, 'There's two of them. Can't just bribe one, it'll have to be both.'

'What's it worth, a crate of ale?' pondered Geoffrey innocently.

'You're joking! Their reputations are on the line here – at least two … each.'

Geoffrey's eyes scanned the garage. 'Frig! How am I going to get four crates of ale?'

'You work there, don't you?' Albert asked slyly. 'The team doesn't have to lose by a mile, perhaps just a technicality…'

As a shaft of streetlight highlighted the furrows on his neighbour's face, Geoffrey thought he saw the devil.

'OK, I'll sort out the beer, you sort the umpires,' he said.

'Deal,' said Albert.

'Cobblers to the cricket,' they whispered as they shook hands.

They peered out from the corner of the garage. Seeing that the coast was clear, Albert dashed inside and Geoffrey tiptoed back towards his house. As he reached the road, he noticed that the light was now on in his lounge. 'Sod it,' he mumbled. 'I'm off for a pint.' As he got out of earshot of the houses, he muttered, 'Technicality. I like that. What a good man.'

Two hours later and mellowing nicely, he entered the front door of his house. This time, all the lights were on and a rich aroma of cooked chicken persuaded his beer-enhanced taste buds that he could manage a portion or two.

'Smells good,' he announced as he walked down the hall.

A surprisingly reassuring reply came from the kitchen. 'Sorry I wasn't here when you arrived home. I thought you might've gone to the pub,' Susan called. Geoffrey looked confused. 'Your case was in the hallway.'

'Curious thing,' Susan remarked, between mouthfuls, as they ate off their knees whilst watching TV.

'What is?' said Geoffrey, not taking his eyes off the screen.

'As I pulled up the drive, I could have sworn I saw two men huddled in next door's garage … in the dark.'

'Nowt to do with me!'

'I didn't say it was.'

'Anyway, you haven't told me why you were so late,' he said, hastily trying to change the subject.

'Another emergency meeting at the cricket club. You wouldn't believe all the work involved. We have to win the game on Sunday, you know.'

'Really,' he replied, trying not to show interest. 'Is everyone well enough now?'

'All, apart from the pro. He's not fit yet.'

'Shame,' said Geoffrey with the wrong intonation.

'We have a replacement, though.'

'Oh, is he any good?'

Another Game Underway

Geoffrey arrived home mid-afternoon and, as usual on home game fixtures, he had to weave through the cars parked down the street. Deep inside, he was bursting to know what plot Albert had engineered in order to halt play. He decided to play his own waiting game.

'Mustn't give anything away and must ignore the temptation to ask "Have you enjoyed yourself? How's the game gone?" Just let it pour out. Whatever happens, don't show any interest at all.' He looked at his watch. 'Bloody hell, another two hours. How on earth can I fill the time?' He laughed as he opened the fridge. 'Better have a beer just like the ones the umpires will have later.'

Albert was also on tenterhooks. He was in the driveway waxing every part of the car to prolong the operation but secretly listening for any hint of an uproar. He noticed a mini-coach cruising up and down. Not thinking it was anything of consequence, he responded positively to his wife's continuous demand for him to go and get his tea.

Halfway through his ham salad, with a mouth full of boiled egg, it happened. The cheers and commotion that erupted from the ground could be heard for miles.

'Yes!' he shouted, as if he had just scored a Cup Final goal, and in the process showered his wife in part-chewed boiled egg.

Geoffrey also heard the cheer and celebrated the yet-unqualified victory of the plot with another beer. During the past hour, he had not been entirely idle. He had practised various consoling expressions in the mirror. 'Don't worry love, there'll be another year,' was the first which he threw out as based on untruth. 'At least we'll be able to sell our house,' seemed a bit crass. 'You'll be able to meet some nice new neighbours,' had him in stitches. So instead he decided to play dumb. 'Say nowt,' he said, mimicking a local accent. Unfortunately, his rehearsals had not prepared him for the events of an hour later.

Reclining on the settee, and surrounded by empty bottles, he was brought back to reality by the entrance of his wife and daughter. Clutching the freezer box, and with a mixture of anger and grief, they clattered their way into the kitchen. The noise of the freezer box being thrown in a corner was immediately upstaged by the sound of Susan ranting.

'Somebody up there doesn't want us to win. Somebody *round here* doesn't want us to win!'

Alison just stood there and wailed. Hearing the commotion, Geoffrey's thoughts raced as best they could in the fog of Old Goat Ale. 'Obviously not gone their way. Now then, what we have here is a rather delicate situation. Not exactly my style, I grant you, but bucketloads of tact required.' He gave it a minute, accurately timed by the clock on the video then, hands in pockets and sporting an exaggerated gait, he strolled into the kitchen.

Ignoring the obvious, he enquired, 'What's up, love?'

Alison had red eyes and Susan's face was streaked with tears.

Almost unintelligibly, Susan explained, 'Game abandoned … girls … babies on pitch … no captain … bat too big … ball too big.'

Geoffrey did not pretend to understand. When in doubt, make a brew. 'You can tell me all about it over a nice cup of tea,' he said.

He turned away quickly to hide a smirk that was creeping to the corners of his mouth. 'Don't smile, for God's sake,' flashed through his mind as he filled the kettle. He turned round but they were busy hanging up their coats. As the water boiled, he looked on. Then Susan stared back and caught him correcting a guilty grin. 'If I thought you had something to do with this…' she said accusingly.

He stirred the contents of the cups then passed one to Susan. 'Charming! I'm sitting here guarding the fort then get accused of doing something I'm not remotely interested in.'

Susan softened, 'I'm sorry, it's just that every time we get an opportunity to save the club, something happens to wreck it.'

'So what's happened this time?' asked Geoffrey, keen to find out.

Susan blew her nose, took a deep breath and explained. 'They batted first. We bowled them out for 170, an easy score to reach. Everybody's excited that a win is on its way. Then the substitute pro comes in and within five minutes, these six girls walk onto the pitch holding babies. As they walk on, they're chanting: "Your baby! Your baby! What you going to do?"'

Geoffrey's expression changed to one of mystified shock.

'He'd only been married a week and his wife was in the seats. She ran out of the ground and he went after her and the girls followed. While all this is going on, one umpire measures the bat and ball with his callipers and the other gets out his tape in the outfield. Then they have a chat and the game's abandoned. We've been accused of cheating and declared losers pending an investigation.'

Geoffrey could hardly contain his admiration for Albert's efforts. 'That's awful,' he sympathised. On the basis that he might give the game away, he changed the subject. 'Biscuit?' he offered as he held a pack of digestives towards his daughter.

Joe Lagg Employs a New Secretary

Since his drunken afternoon and the unceremonious departure of his secretary, Joe Lagg had been finding out just how complicated his own office was and how useless he was at running it. His efforts at independence came crashing down at his first attempt. He could not start the computer, let alone construct a business letter. He even managed to scald the back of his hand while attempting to fill the coffee maker after it had boiled dry. Sitting in his office, sipping muddy coffee and cradling his bandaged hand, he thought it could get no worse.

An instantly recognisable voice echoing from the front of the shop indicated otherwise. 'Hello!' shouted Susan Perkins.

Joe decided to lay low and hope that she would disappear.

'Hello!' she repeated.

Joe sat motionless for a few minutes and presumed she had gone. Then the door opened abruptly. Susan, framed by the white architrave and silhouetted by the bright sunlight, appeared to Joe like the angel of death.

'No, I'm not ready to go yet!' he screamed. He recoiled, foetal-like, to the back of his chair. The sudden movement jolted his cup, resulting in muddy coffee once again being directed by his newspaper into his lap. He stared at her as the warm liquid reached his skin. 'I have no answers for you! I don't know anything, leave me alone!' he shouted, pressing into the back of his chair.

'Calm down,' she said, advancing towards him with a paper towel. 'This is becoming a habit with you,' she smiled as she mopped his desk.

'Don't touch me!' shouted Joe, defending his head with his bandaged hand.

'I'm not going to harm you, I'm here to help you. Let's start by cleaning you up and then you can sign my contract of employment.'

A twitch that had started in Joe's eye on the afternoon he got drunk developed into a full facial movement.

'Fffffrigging joking if you think I'm taking yyyyou on,' he stammered.

'Let's put our cards on the table,' she oozed, making herself comfortable in the chair opposite.

He looked down, unaware she was speaking metaphorically.

'So, how many others have applied?' said Susan, confident that no one else had.

Joe looked up. 'Well none, actually, but I put a big ad in the local paper. Can't understand it…'

Susan rose from the chair, put her hands on her hips and leaned slightly forward. 'The lady you sacked is very bitter. She's telling everyone she meets what a shit employer you are; to quote her, you're a "bullying, hard-faced, chauvinistic bastard". Coffee, proper coffee?'

She left the room and he relaxed his position. Catching his own reflection in a picture on his desk, he noticed his face twitching; he put up his hand to stop it but it continued. He pondered the coffee-stained crossword and tried to focus, but the clues took on a strange angle and then began to rotate faster and faster. He rubbed his eyes but it did not help. The room began to spin; he gripped the sides of the chair, took a deep breath and it began to slow down. Sweat dripped from his brow.

'I feel awful sick,' he moaned. Head in his hands, he tried to rationalise recent events. 'One minute, everything's fine, the next, business is crap, I'm branded a lousy employer, and it's more luck than good judgement that I'm not banged up for murder.'

A voice that he did not recognise suggested, 'Coffee? Fresh, strong coffee?'

The angel of death had changed to the angel of mercy. She moved the papers and placed a steaming cafetière in front of him. He smiled as though he had been rescued from a terrible fate. He watched her fingers grip the round top of the plunger then slowly depress it, until it touched the lid.

She stood and watched as he drooled over the fresh Colombian. He closed his eyes and breathed in the aroma then he looked up with a puzzled expression. 'Mrs Perkins, can I–'

'Susan,' she interjected.

'Susan … I'm not well at the moment, as you can see. I need a break, lot on my mind. I was thinking of closing the shop for a while. Could you come back next week?'

Susan sat on the edge of his desk. 'I have a better idea: you take a few days off and leave the keys. I'll open up for you and make a note of all that happens. It's not good for a business to close … all those missed opportunities.'

He smiled thinly in acknowledgment. 'How come you want to work here? I thought you hated me.'

'I do hate you,' she replied in an inoffensive voice. 'But you need a secretary and I need a job.'

'Oh,' he replied, slightly taken aback.

'Geoffrey's job isn't as secure as we thought. Beer sales have dropped since the poisoning. Happy now?'

He looked up at the ceiling, nodding. He saw the logic of the arrangement but felt he was being manipulated. Yet he also felt as though he could trust her. This worried him but, as he rose and held out the keys, he felt a great weight lift from his shoulders. He walked from the shop as though he were leaving forever.

'How on earth did you manage that?' said Geoffrey to Susan over the evening meal.

'Easy,' she quipped.

'Mind you, I've heard that he's cracking up. He was that pissed the other night, he fell off his stool.'

Susan pushed away her meal and stood up, 'You always belittle the things I do.'

'Susan, I didn't…' His words of explanation were not received.

'Up yours!' she said, raising her middle finger.

First Day, New Job

The following day Susan unlocked the front door of the shop, switched on the lights and put on the kettle. Looking round, she spotted a pile of unopened letters against the wall where the door had swept them. Previously she had been wondering how to fill the day. Now she knew.

Despair Sets In

The season moved speedily on. For the cricket club committee, the prospects of survival were looking increasingly slim.

'After all we've done,' said John Appleby with a sigh. 'Fat chance of winning the league. It's all over. No pro will come here in case they get poisoned.' He slumped in his chair.

The committee members stared at one another across the table, each looking for stimulus, but none was forthcoming.

Arthur looked across at Tom and nodded towards the bar. 'What we need is some lubrication for the wheels of inspiration.'

'Aye. For God's sake, this is more like a bloody wake,' said Tom, rising from his seat.

The rest looked on as they approached the bar. Tom raised the shutters and switched on the bar lights. As the fluorescent bulb flashed into life, he offered a diversion. 'What we have here is the latest offering from Old Goat Brewery. They've kindly donated a barrel free of charge for us to sample and give our opinion.' Tom tapped the pump with his index finger.

Arthur, not convinced, offered an opinion. 'On account of they can't sell it, apparently sales aren't what they should be.' Arthur lined up the beers. 'Pints for men, halves for ladies … it's only fair.'

The problems of the club diminished as they quaffed the ale, then they each gave their own verdict and the probable punter reaction. Fred Pickup's turn came first; imitating a connoisseur, he held his glass to the light, swirled it, took a swig and pronounced, 'We really need to observe the problem from a different angle.'

The others tilted their glasses and stared into the clear liquid.

'No, not the beer, the problem, here in this club. You see, we've been trying to solve the wrong problem.'

Arthur and Tom raised their glasses. 'Works every time. Let me top you up,' said Arthur.

'Go on Fred,' said Janice, eager to hear what he had to say.

'You see, we've been trying to get cash for Benjamin and trying to win a cup to save the club. Really we should be letting Benjamin generate his own money, and then we can concentrate on fixing it so that it doesn't matter if we don't get a cup.'

'Brilliant, what a man!' said Janice, grinning from ear to ear.

'Fine, but how does he generate his own money?' said John, not entirely convinced.

'He can organise the Rasta night, he's always going on about it,' said Susan.

'Frigg's a Rasta night?' Tom whispered into Arthur's ear.

'Not a clue, but it sounds Italian,' Arthur answered.

Fred swilled the beer around again before taking a swig, swallowed, then smiled in acknowledgement. 'The problem of the cup is that it's impossible for us to win one now, so somehow we have to change this ten-year rule.'

John Appleby put down his glass. 'Before we go much further, I'd like to clarify a point.' The others stared in silence. 'This business with the cup, it's nowt to do with Alf Bullock. In fact, he sympathises with us. It's his son, Roland.'

'They're all peeing in the same bucket as far as I'm concerned,' said Tom Deakin accusingly.

'No, it's right,' confirmed Fred. 'After all, it was him who lent us the two grand.'

'Leave this cup business to me,' said Susan softly.

They looked in her direction out of common courtesy, but little credence was given to her words. Tom continued to address the others. 'Another thing … is it me, or do these happenings, poisoning and things, seem more than just accidental occurrences. All them babies … crikey, someone's got to be putting them up to it.'

'Aye, and there's only one man that'll profit from us not winning owt - frigging Roland Bullock,' added John with venom.

The others nodded, but did not add to his statement.

Janice turned to Susan. 'So how do you plan to-?'

Susan stopped her in mid-sentence. 'Just leave it to me,' she replied confidently. Truth was, she had not got a clue. 'Another half please, Arthur,' she added, holding out her glass to change the subject. 'What's it called?' she asked.

Arthur spluttered it out through fits of laughter. 'Old Plodder's Piddle, a commemorative ale to mourn the passing of "Neddy" at Hillside Farm.'

'What's so funny?' pondered Janice.

Susan just shrugged her shoulders.

Later that Evening

Geoffrey had retired for the night and was snoring loudly by the time Susan arrived home. Awakened by the light being switched on, he grumpily asked, 'Good meeting?'

Sitting on the edge of the bed, she turned away, sneered and continued rolling down her tights. 'All this time and I never twigged someone was sabotaging the game,' she added in hushed tones.

Geoffrey, who had started to drift away, suddenly became all ears. 'What ... no ... who?' he stuttered.

'Can't mention names till we're a hundred per cent sure. But we're ninety-nine per cent there already.'

Aided by the beer, Susan fell into a deep slumber as soon as her head hit the pillow. Geoffrey, mind now spinning, did not sleep at all.

The Second Day of the New Job

Susan arrived at her office to find the light flashing on the answerphone. She ignored it until she had made a coffee then, pad and pen at the ready, pressed the playback.

'Susan … Joe here. I've decided I'm going to be off at least a fortnight. I feel like crap. Any problems, use your initiative. Don't call me…'

'Cheeky bastard,' she shouted at the machine.

Meanwhile, up at the Bullock household, Sir Alf was tidying up after making his own breakfast. He was stretching towards the shelf to replace the cups when he heard a voice behind him. 'Let me do that.'

'Flora, I've missed you,' he said, more sincerely than he ever thought possible.

Without any hesitation, she hugged him like a long-lost friend. 'Cup of tea, then I'll tell you all about it,' she gushed.

They sat opposite one another at the kitchen table. Although they had previously been just good friends, to his surprise they automatically held hands across the table. Flora told him about the aromatherapy course she had been on for the past three weeks.

'It was brilliant, all the wonderful effects, cures and feelings that you can imagine.'

'What, from just a smell?' he said, trying not to be negative.

'It's more than just a smell; the oils are taken in by the skin and they affect the whole body, mind and spirit.'

'Curious,' he said, not entirely convinced. 'When I used to get oil on my hands, we were told to wash it off cos it'd do you harm.'

'That was engine oil, this is essential oil,' she replied confidently.

'Engine oil is essential too, you know,' he teased.

'Ah, engine oil, good for the engine, bad for you,' added Flora, trying to put it in simple terms. 'Still no news from your wife then?' she asked, looking round.

'She's gone,' he replied bluntly.

'Gone where?'

'Don't rightly know, she just left a note saying she's going to get some sun,' he sniped.

'On your own then. Are you coping?'

'Coping's a good way to describe it, yes.'

'How's the legs?' she said, grabbing his knee.

'I thought I felt something the other day, you know, a tingle, a shudder.'

'Nothing since?' she asked.

'No,' he said dolefully.

'I'll clean up, then we'll have another brew.'

'OK,' he said, forcing a smile.

During her clean-up, Flora investigated the room she had spotted before she went away. 'Ideal,' she enthused as she closed the door behind her. Over their next tea break, Flora encouraged Sir Alf to go and get some fresh air. 'It's a brilliant day and I need more time to get this place sorted, so you might as well.'

'You sure? Looks bloody cold to me,' he protested.

'Get wrapped up, you'll be OK,' she replied, not taking no for an answer. She smiled and looked him in the eyes as she fastened his seatbelt a little too tight for his comfort.

'Go easy, you'll cut me bloody circulation off,' he remarked as a grin cracked across his face.

He whizzed the wheelchair out onto the lane and up towards the viewpoint. As the breeze flicked his hair, he began to unwind. He stopped between a line of parked cars, took a few deep breaths of fresh air and sighed.

'Is life complicated … or what?' He looked to either side. 'Can't understand it,' he thought. 'Like a row of bloody fish tanks.' Inside the cars, the occupants stared through the misted-up windows caused by the steam billowing from their opened flasks. 'All this way to sit in your car,' he muttered under his breath.

Alongside him, one occupant wiped the window then peered at him.

'Get some fresh air, you'll feel much better,' he mouthed at the onlooker. He looked back across the rolling landscape. 'She was bloody right,' he thought as Flora's words echoed in his head.

On his way back up the drive, he became aware of a change. Something different, but he did not figure it out until he got closer. 'Curtains closed in the middle of the day?'

He got to the front door and a faint flowery smell made him sniff the air like a bloodhound. 'What the hell's she using as polish?'

A bigger shock greeted him as he opened the door. 'Jesus, what have you done?' he said to Flora, who was standing in the hallway in a white smock.

As he peered into the semi-darkness, he spotted candles flickering in tiny pots all the way across the landing on the next floor. He cocked an ear to the faint relaxation music drifting from above. A curious grin emerged on his face. 'What the…!'

'Nothing for you to worry about. Just relax and do as you're told,' she said, trying to keep a straight face.

'I'm not worried, more … baffled.'

They made their way up in the lift and followed the scent of the candles towards the music. She pushed open the door and eased him over the threshold. His face was a picture.

The room was illuminated by night-light candles placed on every surface, all curiously dancing to the rhythm of the relaxation tape. White drapes had been simply but effectively stapled to the walls and ceiling. In the centre of the room, a single bed was covered in white towels.

'Bloody hell, who's being sacrificed?'

'You are, if you don't shut up!' she teased.

She wheeled him in and parked him alongside the bed, and then she cleared her throat even though she did not need to. 'There's no other way to put this, so take your pants down and lie on the bed.'

'That course has done wonders for your brass neck, I'll say that,' he said, startled at her bluntness. 'Shrinking violet when you went away.'

'Just do as you're told … not had a massage before, have you?'

'Never had nowt like this.'

He thought it best to comply, so he slid onto the bed. After undoing his laces, he let his shoes drop to the floor.

'The belt buckle and fly,' she insisted, pointing to his waist.

'I know where it is,' he replied, getting shirty.

The moment he had undone his zipper, she grabbed his turn-ups and without hesitation pulled off his pants. 'Hey up!' he shouted, startled at the swiftness of his de-bagging.

'Just relax and enjoy,' she said while mixing the aromatic oils in a small white dish.

'It'll be difficult, but I'll try.'

As the massage progressed, he found that the enjoyment was being marred by his lack of control of a certain part of his anatomy. The part, unaffected by the paralysis, was indeed responding to the treatment. 'Go easy Flora, you're winding me up.' He started coughing in an attempt to cool things off.

'That's the whole idea. Got to get the blood surging to places it's not been to for a while. Relax,' she reassured him.

'Well you're certainly doing that, it's just that, you know…' Flora followed his eyes, although she knew quite well what he was referring to.

'Oh that, you'll have to do better than that,' she added in a much softer, lower tone. She applied more hot oil to the palms of her hands then massaged the full length of his legs.

'Bloody hell, Flora,' he murmured.

An hour or so later, he was awakened by Flora standing at his side. 'So how do you feel?' she asked softly.

He was wrapped, from his head to his feet, in soft white towelling. 'This has to be heaven,' he enthused. 'Wonderful. I've not felt like this since … come to think of it, I've never felt like this before.' Then he added in a hushed tone, 'Flora, that was brilliant.'

'And we got a result,' she beamed.

He looked puzzled.

'Your legs! They weren't exactly thrashing about, more pulsing and twitching… Coffee's there when you're ready.' She stroked her hand down his legs as she left. 'No hurry,' she added as she closed the door.

The Plot Thickens

Susan sat at her desk, pondering her next move. Having promised to sort out Roland, she was now confronted with how to do it.

'Me and my big mouth,' she thought. Her head swam with plots and theories but nothing seemed plausible. 'Seemed to have it all worked out last night, just dig some dirt then throw it at him, blackmail … easy.'

Staring through the window, she spotted a forlorn canvasser harassing passers-by. 'Eureka,' she said somewhat louder than she intended.

A young mum, carrying her baby and perusing the *For Sale* boards, twitched her nose and grimaced. She shoved her hand down the side of her baby's nappy, tilted her head sideways and mouthed, 'Oh my God.'

'Everything OK?' said Susan.

'Yes, but it's an awful mess down here.'

After lunch, Susan locked the front door and turned the sign to closed. To complete the ruse, she switched off the display lights and went into the back office. Sitting at the desk, she went through her notes again then dialled the number for Bullock Units.

'Is Roland, err... Mr Bullock in?'

'Who's calling?' The secretary was eating her lunch and it sounded as if her mouth was half-filled with sandwich.

Susan's original idea was to remain anonymous but she had not thought of a name. She searched frantically for inspiration. There were only two books on Joe Lagg's desk: a dictionary and a thesaurus. 'It's Miss Roget from *The Throttle Flyer*,' she stuttered.

Susan heard the message being passed on. 'Mr Bullock, there's a lady on the phone, a journalist, foreigner by the sound of it.'

Susan heard the connection click and gripped her notes.

'Miss Roget, what can I do for you?' Bullock said smarmily.

'We're doing a feature on local people in charge of industry, people who are forging a name for themselves as leaders. We wondered if you, as a local entrepreneur, would like to give a comment.'

There was a pause and a loud farting noise as Roland sat up in his chair. Susan heard the noise and shook the phone. 'Mr Bullock … are you there?'

'Well, I'm flattered,' he choked.

'I'll need to take some background details first,' she said, getting the hang of it.

'Recognition, it had to come eventually,' he thought to himself smugly.

'Can we start with your history and education?' Susan made notes furiously as he prattled on. After what seemed like an age, she managed to stop what had developed into a monologue. 'Thank you, Mr Bullock, that'll be fine.'

'Do you need any pictures? When will it be published?' he asked excitedly.

Panic set in. 'Err, soon. Better go now.' Susan replaced the receiver and blew an exaggerated sigh of relief.

Roland was left with the receiver to his ear; it clicked then buzzed. His face remained motionless as he pondered the amateurish finality to the call. His eyes screwed up as the euphoria quickly turned to suspicion. He shouted through to his secretary, 'Get me *The Throttle Flyer*, will you!'

Within seconds, Roland's mind had raced through a list of emotions: excitement, suspicion, disappointment and, finally, humiliation.

'So you don't have a Miss Roget? And you're not doing a piece on local business personalities?' The journalist on the other end burst into laughter. 'I get the message.' Roland held the phone slightly above its rest and let it drop. 'Bastard,' he added to the clatter.

Back in the office, Susan was using directory enquiries to get numbers to fit the names Roland had divulged. She finally thought she was getting somewhere.

'We're planning a party for a former classmate of yours, a Roland Bullock, and we wish to surprise him with a few facts he may have forgotten about… I was wondering if you could help?'

'I don't know about being a mate, but I can certainly tell you a thing or two about him,' said a gruff voice.

'Sounds promising, do you mind if we meet?'

They met the following day at a pub in the nearby village. Jack, a haulier's son, recalled the traumatic experiences of public school education with Roland. After talking to Jack for a while, she got the impression he was not on Roland's Christmas card list. 'So you're not exactly an old chum then?'

'No, he turned out to be a right twat.'

Susan thought it best to come clean. She told him of her plan and was surprised by his response. 'Why didn't you say earlier?' he enthused. 'If it's proper dirt you want, names, places and times, I think we can sort you out. Cost you a pint though.'

She hurried to the bar as Jack cast his mind back to the days of cold showers and corporal punishment.

Later the Same Day

Geoffrey arrived home from work and spotted Albert in his garage. 'Albert … glad I caught you.'

Albert was painting a plastic tub to make it look like a half-barrel, a painful, sacrilegious exercise that, up to two years ago, he would never have contemplated.

'What?' he shouted, objecting to the interruption.

'They know it's you, up at the club, they know what you've been up to.'

'I haven't been up to anything,' said Albert, getting vexed.

'Poisoning … bribery… and all,' Geoffrey stuttered. 'And corruption … in my book that's getting up to a hell of a lot.'

'I had nowt to do with poisoning. Bribery maybe.' Albert paused then leered. 'But you're in it too, right up to your neck. If I go down, I'll take you with me.'

'OK, OK, keep your hair on,' said Geoffrey, twitching nervously. The realisation that he too could be implicated had him pacing back and forth in the garage. 'Is there anything they can pin on us?' he asked anxiously.

'Not unless the umpires split on us, but that incriminates them as well.'

'So what was Susan on about last night? She said they knew who it was.'

'Maybe she's fishing, trying to trip you up? You must have said something in your sleep, or more like when you were pissed. You must be pissed every night. Dustmen complain like hell about carrying away your empties.'

'Nowt to do with you, my drinking habits are my business. I'll have you know it's me that's keeping the firm going.'

'Going bust from what I hear,' snapped Albert, a laugh mixing in with his words.

Geoffrey faced him nose to nose. 'You're a snidey bastard at heart, aren't you?'

Albert looked at the ground. 'I didn't mean it, it just comes out.'

'I'll do some asking round, see what I can come up with,' said Geoffrey, setting off home.

'Drop us in it and you want stuffing!' cussed Albert.

'Have some faith,' were Geoffrey's final words.

'Last bloke who had faith got crucified,' Albert muttered, grabbing the brush.

Tentative Enquiries During Breakfast

'You know the other night,' said Geoffrey, doing his best but giving an unconvincing impersonation of someone who was not bothered about the reply.

'Yes,' said Susan.

'Did I hear you say that you knew who was responsible for the poisoning … and things?'

'You did,' she replied, giving nothing away.

'So who is it then?' he asked outright, as his curiosity got the better of him.

'What's it to you?'

'Just being nosy.' Seeing he was getting nowhere, he decided on a different tack. 'Our beer sales have slumped since the poisoning.'

'But you've been cleared!'

'Ah, but folk are queer like that. No smoke without fire and all that.'

'Get Alison to school or she'll be late. We'll continue this later.'

Geoffrey did as instructed, but somewhat unwillingly. As soon as he had gone, Susan got out her notepad. 'Responsible for bankrupting the brewery,' she said as she wrote.

Later that day, she phoned Roland. 'Bullock Units, can I help?' said the robotic voice of the secretary.

'Hello, it's Miss Roget from *The Flyer*. Is Mr Bullock in?'

The secretary immediately put her hand over the receiver and whispered loudly, 'It's that woman from *The Flyer*.'

'Put her on,' said Roland. He prepared himself by sitting upright in his chair. 'Miss Roget, I didn't expect to hear from you again so soon,' he said.

'Mr Bullock, something's cropped up. We're doing another feature about the impending demise of the local cricket club and we wondered if you'd like to comment?' Silence from Roland. 'Shall I take that as "no comment"? Well, we are doing another feature on pupils who were *comforted* by their tutors at school, would you like to comment on that then? Are you still there, Mr Bullock, or should I call you *Master Bollock*?'

Roland let the receiver drop onto the rest. Sitting back in his chair, he could feel sweat dampening his shirt. 'What a nasty piece of goods,' he murmured.

'Something wrong?' said the secretary, poking her head round the door.

'I think one of my skeletons slipped out for a walk.'

She did not reply, just twisted her face in puzzlement.

Susan sat with the phone buzzing at her ear for a moment. 'How would he react? He wouldn't just change the ten-year rule – that'd be too easy. He would lose face. Violence, perhaps?' She pondered about Roland's state of mind.

Moments later, she found out. The phone rang; she stared at it uneasily, her hand poised above it, and then the answering machine clicked in. After the recorded message, she froze as she heard Roland's voice. 'Meet me at the Ram Inn at seven. Bring the brothers. We have a little problem to solve.'

***

Later, unaware that the intended person did not receive his message, Roland drove to the pub, ordered a drink and sat alone at a table. He kept an eye on the door in anticipation of Joe and the brothers. Distracted, he did not notice the woman sitting at a nearby table; if he had looked closer, he would have noticed she was wearing a hat, scarf and overcoat even though it was a warm evening. He ordered another drink then looked at his watch. He reached into his pocket for his phone. This time he dialled Joe Lagg's mobile number.

'Where the hell are you?' he hissed.

'In bed, off sick, flu, or sommat. Where are you?' Joe said nasally.

'I'm in the pub waiting for you. Don't you listen to your answerphone?'

'I've told you, I'm off sick,' Joe said weakly.

'Sick or not, we have to talk, urgently. I'm not prepared to go over it on the phone.' As he spoke, he noticed the over-dressed woman near the window and focused on her. 'Tomorrow. Fine, in here then. The brothers too, don't forget.'

He looked at his phone then glanced back to where the woman had been sitting; she had gone, leaving her drink untouched. 'Who's the woman in the window seat?' he asked the barman.

'Never seen her before.'

Roland pondered a moment. 'Another whisky please … hell of a day.'

The same sentiment was going through Susan's mind as she left. 'Just a weeny bit too close for comfort,' she said to the pavement as she kept her head down.

Next day, she decided to take a rest. 'No espionage, no lying phone calls, just a normal working day like everyone else,' she thought. But a phone call, mid morning, from the local planning officer cut short her 'normal day'.

'Is Mr Lagg in?' he asked.

'He's off sick. He's left me in charge, can I help?'

'Probably not. There are a few queries about the outline planning permission for the houses going up on the old cricket ground,' he said casually.

'The cricket ground?' she repeated.

'Yes, you must know it, Throttle Cricket Club just up the road from you.'

'Of course, I know where it is. I live on the edge of it,' she said, getting agitated.

'Apparently it's not being used any more,' he added coolly.

'Of course it's bloody used, there's a game on this weekend,' Susan shouted. She hung up the phone, then ushered the browsing customers out of the shop. 'Sorry, it's an emergency! We have to close.'

'Don't know how you make a do,' said a disgruntled gent, banging the door behind him.

Susan closed down the shop and sat at her desk, reading the sheet in front of her. She went over her script then dialled Roland's number. Getting straight through to him threw her off balance.

'Ah, Miss Roget, I've been waiting for your call.'

'Oh,' she said with a tremble in her voice.

'Let's put our cards on the table. I know you don't work at *The Flyer* and it's unlikely that Roget is your real name. Am I right so far? So what exactly are you up to?'

Susan was dumbstruck. 'Bastard,' she thought.

'I haven't got all day, so if you'd like to get to the point, maybe we can come to an understanding.'

She exploded. 'Understanding! With you? You underhanded weasel!'

'Steady on,' he replied calmly.

Irrationally, she thought it time to declare her hand. 'I'm a friend of the cricket club, the one that you intend to build on, and we know that you're responsible for-'

'Ah, it's *we* now. So there's more than one of you?' he jibed. 'You can't prove a thing, so if you've got nothing more to add, I've got to go.' He pulled the receiver away from his ear, but he could still hear Susan ranting on the other end.

'I'll see to it that everyone knows about your schooldays and the business with the tutors, and what they used to call you if … if…'

'If what?'

'If you don't cancel your plans to knock down the cricket club.'

He paused, and then said calmly, 'Now look lady, whoever you are. Number one: I do not believe you would go as far as to slander me for fear of going to court. Number two: plans are already in place to ensure that the cricket club loses its ground in accordance with the rule book. OK?' He put down the phone.

On the other end of the line Susan was stunned. She tried to remain calm but it was impossible. 'I ought to put his windows in at least,' she thought.

She sat, head in hands, for what seemed like ages. She could not be bothered re-opening the shop so she had another coffee and left. As she approached her house, she spotted Albert in his garage. He was painting more barrels.

'Hello Albert,' she said, but either he did not hear or he was ignoring her. She blew into the air. 'Sod you then,' she thought, and went into the house. She went through various strategies but they all implicated her immediately or seemed doomed to failure from the start. She watched from the kitchen window as Albert put his paint away. And then a plan emerged.

***

The following morning Roland swerved into the car park, then skidded his car to a halt when he saw the three-foot-high sketch of a part of male anatomy that he thought he had left behind in his schooldays.

His secretary, who had been in before him, told him what she had done. 'I thought you'd want me to get the police in and ever such a nice bobby came. He didn't stop long though, said he had other artists to chase–'

'Do you want me to be a bloody laughing stock? Phone *The Flyer*, why don't you! Phone the police back and tell them to cancel their enquiries!'

Roland slammed the door as he headed towards his desk. 'I'll have her bleeding guts for this, Miss Soddin' Roget.'

Minutes later, the secretary pushed open the door. 'They've got a suspect in custody, a man.'

Roland put his head in his hands. 'It's a woman, a woman has done this.'

'The security video's a bit fuzzy,' said the secretary, trying to be helpful.

'Oh never mind. If *The Flyer* rings, tell them "no comment". Have you organised a painter?'

The Local Nick

'The paint used for the graffiti matches the one you've used on your barrels, even the brush matches … very clever,' the detective sniggered. 'It's fairly common knowledge what you think of Mr Bullock and his cricket club, so why don't you just own up, Mr Bradley, and save us all some time?'

A constable, previously at attention, started to laugh. 'Yes, constable, can we share your joke?'

The constable did his best to maintain his composure as he revealed, in courtroom fashion, his discovery. 'Just made the connection, sir. It's clearly a play on words. The graffiti on the doors and the name of the owner of the company have, how shall we say, an unfortunate spelling correlation.' At that point he was asked to leave for fear of lowering the tone of the proceedings.

Geoffrey arrived home early to find Mrs Bradley in a state. 'They've taken him away,' she wailed.

'Whose taken who where?'

'The police, they've taken Albert to the station.'

'What for?'

'They wouldn't say, but it must be serious.'

'How do you make that out?'

'A policeman put his hand on his head as Albert was put in the car. I've seen it on the telly and they always do that to suspects when it's serious.'

Susan arrived home to find Geoffrey sitting at the kitchen table. 'Bloody hell,' she remarked. 'You look like you've seen a ghost!'

'They've arrested Albert, they took him away this morning.'

The coat she had partly removed fell to the floor. 'What for?' she asked, louder than she intended.

'Don't know. Thought you'd know more about it than me – you said you know who's behind the goings on at the club.'

'We do know, but it's got nothing to do with Albert.'

'Oh,' said Geoffrey, feeling better. 'So what on earth's he been arrested for?'

'How the hell do I know!' snapped Susan.

Later that evening, Geoffrey and Susan were settling down in front of the TV when a knock at the front door disturbed their 'quality leisure time'. 'I'll get it,' Geoffrey muttered. 'Albert! Come in, we've been worried about you.'

Susan leapt out of her chair and entered the hallway. Albert remained in the doorway, under the light.

'Somebody's set me up,' he snarled. 'Last night someone borrowed my paint and brush and used it to paint slogans on Roland Bullock's door. And whoever it was also borrowed my old coat and hat to do it in. Lucky for me, there was a security video; it is a poor picture, but the expert said that whoever it was, they were much smaller than me. They also said, how shall I put it, that it looked like a woman's figure.' His eyes widened as he stared at Susan.

'Who'd do a thing like that? Must be someone with a grudge,' Susan sniffed.

'Fancy a beer, Albert?'

'A couple, more like. Can't stand many more days like today. My whole life has been flashing by. At one point this afternoon, clear as day, I could see my photo on the front of the tabloids,' he said. The glass of beer that had been pushed into his hand was trembling.

Behind Freshly Painted Doors

'I'm afraid something's cropped up. We tried to contact your colleague, Mr Lagg, but he was unavailable…' Mr Trafford, the bank manager, was on the phone.

Roland sensed trouble in his voice. He sat back in his chair. 'Oh?' he said impatiently.

'On the proposal. You indicated that the land was no longer in use. However, a few enquiries have indicated that this is not the case. In fact, our sources advise us that the land may never be available for building.'

'Oh?' repeated Roland, even more impatiently.

'As a lender in the locality, we have to be careful about our reputation. If we're seen to be jumping the gun on an issue like this, borrowers may vote with their feet. Lending is a cut-throat business these days, lots of competition-'

'Stop!' Roland shouted down the phone. 'Are you going to put up the money or do I have to go somewhere else?'

'You'll get the same reaction wherever you go. You're free to shop around, of course.'

'Stop right there!' Roland barked.

'We may be in a better position to do business when the land is no longer used for its present purpose. Feel free to get in touch when-'

'Yes, thanks for the advice.' Roland hung up then addressed the empty room. 'In that case, we'll have to speed things up,' he growled.

Up to No Good

Mrs Williamson looked out of the kitchen window towards the wooden shed beyond the vegetable patch. A feeble yellow light emitted from it. 'What does he get up to in there?' she wondered, without taking her hands out of the sink.

'He'll be messing with his bike,' her husband replied from behind his paper.

'Well I don't like it. He spends far too long down there.'

'Leave the lad alone, you should be grateful.'

'Grateful? It's not natural! He's sitting there in the pitch dark,' she shrieked.

'Gloom, yes, but not pitch dark. Look, the lad is down there in the shed, pottering with his bike. We know where he is and, as far as we know, he's not up to mischief. Be bloody grateful for that.'

'Suppose so, but I'm not keen,' she said with resignation.

Unfortunately, Mr Williamson's reassurances were misplaced. As they sat down to watch the round of evening soaps, young Master Williamson was plotting sinister retribution.

He had been simmering for months since he was dropped from the cricket team and the humiliation at the meeting in the local hall served only to heighten his desire to get even. He had ventured back to the pitch once or twice for practice sessions, but the ribbing from established players was too much. So now, most evenings he sat in the shed by candlelight and dreamt of nasty happenings for John Appleby, club chairman and selector for the second team. He had come up with several plots, only to bottle out on grounds that they were too scary;

and, of course, since his very public shaming, he would be prime suspect. However, since the poisoning, he considered it an opportunity not to be missed.

'I might just be able to add to his suffering,' he said through gritted teeth as he stuck pins in a whittled effigy.

***

The following day, dust filled the air as the cricket club committee cleaned and polished.

'Do you know what some bastard did last night?' said John Appleby. He and Tom Deakin were sweeping the clubhouse in preparation for the forthcoming Rasta Night. Tom shook his head.

'There I was, sitting down to me supper, when there was a hell of a racket on the front door so I opened it, and this huge ball of newspaper was on fire.'

''Kin' hell!' Tom sympathised.

'Scorched the bleeding door,' John added. Tom stopped his sweeping in astonishment. 'So I stamped it out with my foot, like you would.'

'Aye,' Tom concurred.

'And do you know what? It were a parcel of dog shit, all over me bleeding slippers. Set fire to me turn-ups, then I walked it all up the hall. Wife played bloody hell.' At this point Tom doubled over, hardly able to breathe for laughing. 'If I ever get my hands on the bastards, I'll wring their bleeding necks.'

Tom tried to be sympathetic but the vision of John stamping on the newspaper had him holding his aching sides, and he had to walk away.

'Hello … problem?' asked Janice.

Tom just pointed in John's direction and carried on laughing.

Game Underway

Two rather elderly and battered single-decker buses pulled up outside the ground. The occupants, mostly young men with shaved heads, heavily tattooed arms and wearing ex-army clothing, marched towards the clubhouse. At the same moment, Tom Deakin sidled up alongside an old adversary, an ex-player who was there to support the opposing team.

'How the hell are you?' he asked out of politeness.

'Fettling,' said the man of few words.

'See you've brought some support.'

'Nowt to do with us. Thought they were yours.'

'Don't look like supporters, more like rent-a-mob on a day out.'

'Mmmm,' he speculated.

Tom followed them into the pavilion and found them queuing at the bar. John approached. 'Have you seen the outfits? Anarchy international, if you ask me!'

'Then we better keep them happy,' Tom said. Reaching for the phone, he dialled the number of the brewery.

'Hello, Tony? Look, if you want to shift some of that beer of yours, get your van loaded up and get down here quick. Two coachloads have turned up and they look like they've got a thirst on.'

The coach party settled themselves on the grass, and then it was a steady trek between the bar and the gents. About four o'clock, a transit van arrived and three similarly dressed but smarter gentlemen climbed out. They peered across the ground until they spotted their troops sitting on the grass alongside the sight screen. They marched at double time towards them.

'Soddin' going on here?' one of them barked, as though on a parade ground.

'Following orders, sir,' said a voice from the back.

The man with the sergeant-major presence leaned forward awkwardly and in a loud whisper told his troop what he thought. 'This place should be a mass of devastation by now. Your orders were to infiltrate the ground then stop the game by any means,' he hissed.

'We're still on the "infiltrate" bit,' heckled one of the mob drunkenly. The others laughed uncontrollably.

'Insubordination of the highest order. You'll all be on a charge,' the sergeant major threatened.

'Piss off,' replied a voice from the centre of the group.

'Who said that?'

'Chill out! The beer's grand,' came back the advice.

'He's right you know, best I've tasted for a long while,' added his sidekick, who had not refused when handed a pint.

Seconds later, the small crowd erupted. 'Jesus! Did you see that? He knocked it clean out t'ground?' shouted an enthusiast.

The sergeant major tried again. 'Charges, all of you! Do you hear?' He was getting into full swing with his orders and threats when he realised he had become the focus of attention of every spectator and one very irate chap in a white smock.

The umpire, who had walked over to where he was standing, offered some advice, 'Sit thy down you bloody idiot, you're holding the bloody game up.'

Sheepishly the sergeant major sat amongst his squad. 'You're for it when we get back,' he seethed.

As the day continued the group, including the drivers, mellowed happily. The combination of Old Plodder's

Piddle, the hazy afternoon sun and Janice Hinchcliffe's meat pie and peas removed their rent-a-mob mentality and replaced it with a more laid-back approach. Co-ordination and speech became a problem, so they just pointed at their open mouths when ready for a refill.

After the game finished, an elected representative (the only one left with the power of speech) addressed John Appleby, who had walked out onto the ground. He stood as best he could, resisting the strong desire to fall over. Then, after taking a deep breath, he spoke as though his brain could only cope with two or three words at a time.

'Brilliant day … goosed now … no drivers … all pissed … no way home … what d'you think?'

'I think you're buggered lad,' John said bluntly. 'Mind you, night's only just beginning. We've a Rastafarian night starting in…'

The representative grinned, shuffled back to his mates and related what he had heard. 'Buggered … beginning … boozing … a vegetarian fight … in an hour.'

'Must be throwing friggin' spuds at one another.'

The home side achieved a close-fought victory; it no longer affected the outcome of the league but it did provide the basis for a rapturously intoxicating night. Janice went home to get changed and returned clutching the Saturday evening edition of *The Throttle Flyer*. She was sporting a broad grin. 'Have you seen this?' she asked Fred gleefully.

'Famous at last!' Fred shouted to John, who was only just within earshot. He waved the paper in the air and tried again. 'You're in the paper! A star is born,' he mocked.

'Where's Tom?' John said angrily as he read the headline: *Blaze Hero Puts Foot In It.*

By eight-thirty, the club was thumping to the musical beat provided by Benjamin. He had brought his Bob Marley collection and, as the night wore on, the guests mimicked his accent and the way he moved. The coach party, now sporting bright-red faces, remained on the grass to cool their sunburn. As they swayed, they looked like a clump of giant tulips in the breeze. Two members of the troupe, whose conversation was now almost incoherent, pondered their predicament. Eyes wandering wildly, and having little or no control over their mouths, they communicated very slowly.

'We gonna sit 'ere all neet?'

'If tha wants.'

'I'll have to go, but Ah can't get up'

'Get driver to tek us 'ome?'

'I am the feckin' driver.'

'Oh, well, if we can't get 'ome, it must be time for another.'

They tried to help each other up but their legs were in a worse state than their mouths.

'Whose round is it?'

'Whoever can stand, I'd say.'

They grinned, then whispered, and then grinned again. 'Ants, ants, big red ants!' they shouted.

A comrade, who was only perhaps one per cent less drunk, scrambled to his feet. 'Your round, your round!' they shouted and pointed.

Inside the club, the low lighting and atmospheric beat of the Rasta music was having a hypnotic effect on the crowded dance floor. Benjamin was fascinated; he was able to control their movements and their voices. As the tempo and temperature rose, he felt he could control their minds. He was under the impression that the majority, mainly women, would have followed him to the ends of the earth – or at least to the nearest patch of long grass.

At the bar, the conversation revolved around the quality of the beer, the convivial social atmosphere and the fact that within months it would all be gone. The anger at the injustice of the situation was reaching lynch-mob proportions.

'What gives him the right to take this off us?' argued Arthur. He waved his arms about to indicate the size of the building but, as he was still holding a pint of beer, all he managed was to soak them all through. The circle of friends nodded approval and backed away.

As Susan retreated she backed, as though pre-arranged, into Tom Deakin. 'Can I have a word?' he said mysteriously.

'What's your problem?' she replied uneasily.

They stepped away from the circle. 'Well actually, it's not my problem,' he coughed.

She looked at him blankly. 'Come on, say your piece.'

He rummaged in his pocket then produced what in the dimness of the disco lights looked like a small discarded piece of cloth. 'I believe these are yours. You left them in the shed.'

The low lighting not only concealed the petite article of underwear, but also the reddening of her face. 'How do you know they're mine? Could be anybody's,' she said, almost stunned into silence.

'Give me some credit,' Tom replied bluntly, and walked away.

Susan deftly stuffed the skimpy item, especially bought for the occasion, back in her bag. 'Think positive,' she muttered. 'Thought I'd lost them.'

Around midnight, Roland cruised past in his car and was shocked to see the revelry continuing. He reached for his mobile phone. Modern technology has created the ability to make immediate contact with others all around the world, but this is based on a simple premise that they are willing and able to accept your call. Roland was only a hundred yards away from the person he wished to speak to but the premise had failed. He could have walked up to where the phone was ringing but the phone's melodic bleep was rendered ineffective beneath the comatose body of the leader of rent-a-mob who was where he had been most of the day, lying on the grass.

Roland waited a while then spun the rear wheels of his car as his patience gave out. He headed to his office and decided to get some inspiration from a bottle of ten-year-old malt. The more he drank, the greater was his desire to sort this matter out.

Aided by alcohol-induced courage, he returned to the cricket club in the early hours, this time on foot and carrying a can of petrol.

The pavilion was a wooden structure supported by a three-layer row of bricks, with one in every ten removed to provide a through-flow of air. Roland made a funnel from some old cardboard and poured the petrol through the gaps in the bricks. The petrol soaked into the mass of litter and dried grass that had accumulated over the years. He systematically worked along one end then across the back and finally along the other end. For fear of being seen, he decided against dousing the front.

'Too risky. Always be some bastard who can't sleep,' he said under his breath.

When he had finished, he put the lid on the can. To his horror he discovered that, in his efforts to do the job quickly, he had also doused his shoes, socks and trousers in petrol. A vision of himself in a ball of flame flashed through his mind; he even saw the ironic headline: *Arsonist Burned Alive. Clubhouse Saved.*

'No option,' he thought as he removed his trousers.

He rummaged in his pockets for the matches, placed his neatly folded trousers under a hedge, and then crept back barefoot to the walkway between the shed and the clubhouse. He was building up the nerve to strike the match when he heard voices from inside the shed. He dropped the unlit match and held his breath. After a moment, curiosity got the better of him. He gingerly moved over to the shed and put his ear to the door. The noises from within puzzled him.

'Wha, wha, ooh, ooh, Jesus Christ.'

'Religious meeting at this hour, in a garage?' Roland mused.

'Oh, good God!' the voice continued.

Even more intrigued, Roland edged closer. He was not to know that the rusty metal door was not quite shut; as he pressed his ear against it, the door clanged against its metal frame. Fearing discovery and using his old maxim 'leg it while you can', he set off across the pitch. But legging it across the pitch was not one of his best ideas.

Even though it took Benjamin only a few seconds to disentangle himself from his latest conquest, he still had time to spot the half-naked figure before it disappeared down the road. 'Bare-arsed streaking across the pitch? Usually they do it during the game,' he said to the female, who had now gone off the idea of a shed full of tools doubling as a bedroom.

The commotion roused one of the rent-a-mob crew, who was shivering with cold having crashed out for the night on the grass. 'A piss, another beer and a warmer place to doss. Simple necessities,' he muttered as he headed towards the pavilion.

The lock on the door was a trivial matter for someone who could break into a Land Rover 4x4 in ten seconds. Having satisfied his first priority, he stumbled in the darkness towards the bar – only to find it shuttered up. 'More subtlety required for this,' he said, smashing a chair through one of the flimsy hardboard sections.

He flicked the light switch behind the bar. As the fluorescent light flickered on, his eyes were dazzled by the display of so many different ways of poisoning his liver. Not wishing to mix his intake, he pulled the lever on the beer pump but nothing happened. Disappointment then elation swept over his face as he spotted a door marked 'cellar'. He pushed it open, put his hand round the corner, felt for the light switch and flicked it on. It was the last movement he made under his own effort. The petrol fumes had filled the cellar. It was only a small spark from the old light switch but it was enough to ignite the explosion that both spiritually and physically transported him heavenward. A split second before he expired, he could not believe his rotten luck.

A few hours later, the cold light of day displayed the full effects of the blast. A pile of smouldering rubble was all that remained. Onlookers watched the firemen prod the hot bricks and charred wood. Meanwhile, a lone policeman, notebook at the ready, scribbled statements.

'Thought it were gonna take off. All this flame from underneath, it actually lifted off the ground,' said a female witness who wished to remain anonymous.

'Gas leak,' said a fireman.

'Aye, got to be gas,' confirmed another.

'No soddin' gas on,' said John Appleby, first of the committee to arrive.

'Oh ... right,' said the fire chief.

'Rotten stink, is it beer or petrol?'

'Mmm ... not quite sure. They both smell alike and have the same effect,' said John, trying to make light of the situation.

A fireman in the middle of the rubble poked something soft. As he prodded harder, the end of his stick took on a crimson colour. 'Think we 'ave a casualty,' he announced.

The policeman looked up, flipped over another page in his book and moved closer.

Within minutes the area was cordoned off, blue lights flashed and where previously there had been little interest, it now seemed as though every blade of grass would be investigated.

As John stared in disbelief, Craig Williamson approached on a brand-new bike. He bravely cycled clean across the pitch. 'Bit of a mess,' he said, grinning from ear to ear.

John turned round and immediately put two and twenty-two together.

Across the way, the Bradley and Perkins families surveyed their blast-affected bungalows. Albert raised his hands in despair. 'Can you believe it? Put mesh up to save the windows from a ball and an explosion puts the whole bloody lot in. I don't think we're insured for terrorist attack.'

'Terrorist attack?' queried his wife.

'Place was full of anarchists yesterday. Two coachloads. It'll be them as planted the bomb.'

Geoffrey deliberated. 'But why the cricket club?'

Just then, Susan ran over from the pitch. 'They've found a body in the rubble, one of them lads off the coach.'

'What did I say? It probably went off as he was planting it,' said Albert.

His wife turned to him, highly embarrassed. 'Shut up you fool,' she said and promptly dragged him inside.

Alison clutched at Geoffrey's leg. 'Daddy, I don't like it here any more.'

He looked down at her, picked her up and carried her away from the remains of the front door. 'Me neither, love. That's why we're having a few days away while they fix this lot.'

The Treatment Continues

The aromatherapy cure for Sir Alf's incapacity was working, but only slowly.

'Have to increase the reps, the intensity and maybe change the oil,' advised Flora.

'Suits me. What are reps?' he asked as he swung himself on the bed.

As the massaging and relaxing music got underway, Sir Alf and Flora drifted into their own thoughts, unaware of a taxi making its way up the drive.

Miriam paused just before opening the door. She peered up at the sky: it had clouded over. Although it did not look like rain, it was cold and damp. She wondered why she had come back. Only a few hours ago, she was bathed in the clear blue sky and sunshine of Majorca. In fact, this very taxi had taken her to Manchester Airport just four weeks ago. Totally hacked off with the goings-on at home, she responded to a bronzed middle-aged lady's advice at her health club: 'The sun, sea, red wine and the Spaniards … it'll take years off you. Just bugger off before you think too hard about it.'

So she had buggered off. She left a note giving little detail of her intentions, just saying, 'I'm going away'. She also followed the other bit of advice: 'Tek nowt but your credit card.'

It was an early morning flight. 'Even better,' she thought as she quietly closed the front door. 'Less explaining to do.'

She felt odd going away and not having to carry a case. 'Just passport, tickets and Visa card,' she muttered as she checked her handbag for the third time. She had asked the taxi driver to pick her up at the end of the drive and, as she walked away from the house, she felt like she was escaping. It was a good feeling, exciting, if a little weird.

The flight was shorter than she anticipated; there was just time for a coffee, a glance at the duty free and then the announcement came that they were about to land. She noticed during the flight that while the cloud cover was very thick over the UK, it was clear as a bell across the Channel.

'No wonder we're all depressed and they're all happy,' she said to the woman sitting next to her. Her fellow passenger offered a simpering smile of acknowledgement over the top of a thick novel.

As Miriam stepped out of the plane and made her way down the steps, she noticed that everyone was smiling. 'Amazing what a bit of sun does.' She felt uplifted as she made her way through the Nothing to Declare gate and couldn't resist a comment. 'Could tell you a thing or two,' she said to the uniformed guard who totally ignored her.

What really made her day was when she saw her name on a placard being held aloft by a very smooth and tanned young man. She felt elated. She let him prattle on as they drove to the hotel, whilst she stared through the window.

The scenery of steep valleys and quaint villages fascinated her. The driver casually screeched down the narrow roads that all seemed to have perilous drops into the sea. Although she had fastened the safety belt, she clung on to the straps.

'Slow down, for God's sake, unless you want my breakfast all over your seats!' she barked at the driver. He spoke little English but he got the message from the terror and volume of her voice.

She had booked the accommodation out of the *Bijou and Friendly* brochure but was a little apprehensive. As she pointed out to the travel agent, 'Do I read "tiny and overbearing" for bijou and friendly?'

The driver turned off the main road and freewheeled downhill, then straight into the cobbled courtyard of an old but well-kept hotel. 'It's bloody gorgeous,' Miriam said as she paid the taxi driver.

She wandered to the end of the courtyard, through a stone archway and looked out over the rocky shoreline. She shaded her eyes from the bright sun and saw small yachts circling the island. Following a path sheltered by orange and lemon trees, she wandered towards a private pool with a small bar. As she approached, a waiter anticipated her thoughts. 'Fresh orange juice with ice?'

'Grand,' she concurred.

The waiter, who had not come across this expression before, tilted his head. Luckily, a voice from behind her interpreted. '*Si, por favor.*' The interpreter held out his hand in welcome. 'Mrs Bullock?' he said in a Middle English accent.

Miriam hesitated at the formality, then gushed, 'What a place you've got here.'

They chatted and exchanged pleasantries, and then the host suggested, 'Can I help you with your luggage? You must be tired after your journey.'

She looked at the table, slightly embarrassed; she had taken her friend's advice literally. 'It's like this …'

At the very moment that she hesitated, he put his index finger to his lips. 'You don't have to explain anything to me. You're here to relax and enjoy yourself. It's my duty to see that everything's in place for that to happen.' Then he smiled in a way that Miriam thought was very sincere.

He showed her to her room and opened the balcony double doors. 'I thought you might appreciate a sea view,' he said.

She looked round at the sumptuous furnishings; it was everything she had tried to create at home.

'I must go out to buy some essentials,' she said as she opened the walk-in wardrobe.

'Ah,' he said, looking at his watch. 'The shops will all be closed now.' Then he smiled again, 'That kind of shopping usually takes place in the evening when the sun cools and the lights go on. It's a much better atmosphere. Can I get one of the ladies in our employ to show you the best shops?'

Miriam hesitated. 'I'd much prefer if you could accompany me. Would you mind? You seem to have such good taste.'

'It'd be my pleasure. In the meantime, relax; there are towelling robes for your use. If you'd like a snack, the waiter will organise it for you.'

After he had gone, she lay back on the king-sized bed and stared up at the chandelier. 'Am I dreaming or what?' she whispered.

It took a few days for her to acclimatise and find her way around. She tested the bus and taxi service and decided that the public transport was fine. 'I'm not in any rush, so what's it matter how long it takes?' she thought as she tried to fathom the bus timetable. She bought a large straw hat from the market. It was larger than most and a trifle colourful, but she felt fine. 'Couldn't get away with this at home,' she told the lady as she handed over the money. The lady smiled, not having understood a single word.

She was strolling by the shore, wearing the big hat and a flowing sarong from the same market, when she realised that she was not angry any more. She felt relaxed for the first time in years.

Each day she took the bus further afield. 'So much to see,' she said to Arthur, the host, when they planned her next excursion. She enjoyed the quaint markets and matched each trip to market day in a different town.

'Do be careful, there are people who frequent markets who prey on, how shall I say, affluent individuals such as you. They pick your pockets, sell you fakes and misuse your Visa card. Never let it out of your sight,' Arthur warned.

She felt the warmth of his concern. 'Thanks for looking out for me, I do appreciate it.' As she spoke, she inadvertently placed her hand on his knee. He smiled and put his hand on top of hers.

As she ventured further and further away, so her return to the hotel became later. One day she arrived back after the evening meal.

'Tell me to mind my own business if you like but…' Arthur paused as he offered her a glass of red wine. 'I worry … a lady on her own … not familiar with the area… Would you mind if I give you this?' he pushed a small mobile phone towards her.

'Oh Arthur, you do look after me.'

'It lights up,' he enthused. 'So you can see what you're doing.'

In the fading light, the phone shone in her hand. 'You'll have to show me how to use it.'

'I'll take that as a yes,' he said. 'You must be hungry?'

'I thought dinner had finished?'

'It's OK. I'll prepare a typical Spanish dinner for us.'

'Can I help? I used to work in a kitchen … twenty-five years ago.' They went into the kitchen. 'Size of them pans,' she enthused.

'Paella pans,' he answered. He reached for a smaller double-handed pan that was clean on the inside but looked on the outside like it had been rescued from a house fire.

'Paella for two?'

'Right then,' she said, donning an apron.

They took the plates of rice, chicken and seafood and sat on the plastic chairs that surrounded the pool. He beckoned the waiter and spoke to him in Spanish. Minutes later, the waiter returned with an ice bucket containing, as he described it 'a local vintage modelled after my physique, smooth and well rounded.' Miriam laughed heartily as his dry humour continued throughout the meal.

'Do you know, I haven't laughed like this in years,' she said.

As the humour subsided, Arthur ordered another bottle. 'Your Spanish is so good,' she enthused.

'You have to practise. If you can't speak the lingo, you either starve or pay a fortune for everything.'

'How long have you been practising?'

'Fifteen years.'

'You've been here fifteen years?' she said with disbelief.

'I've been in worse places,' he responded.

'On your own?'

'Came out with my wife. We bought this place as a wreck – took ages to do it up. That was our undoing. She went back home after two years, couldn't stand the building work, left me to it. When it was finished she wanted a divorce and half of what the hotel was worth. Well, by that time, it was worth a few bob but I had no option but to get a loan or sell up. Glad I didn't. Tell me about you,' he said as he topped up their glasses.

Miriam took a deep breath. 'Good God, where do I start?' she pondered.

'Here,' he said, holding out his glass. 'To you and your holiday.'

They touched glasses and she toasted, 'To you and your idyllic hotel.'

He listened intently and they kept eye contact as she explained how the past twenty-odd years had been 'a disappointment, to say the least'. He refilled her glass at an opportune moment.

'Am I going on too much?' He did not speak, just smiled and shook his head. 'So you see,' she said as she finished, 'what I've had to put up with.'

'How on earth could he ignore your needs, your charm?' Arthur said smoothly.

'Do you know, I've had these thoughts running round in my head for years. Not once have I found anyone I could tell and I've only known you for a few days.'

'The Spanish air,' he laughed. 'It works wonders for your tongue.'

'Not only your tongue.' She pushed forward the key to her room. 'This duty of yours, how far does it go?'

Back to Reality

'Don't go away,' she ordered the taxi driver.

Leaving her bags on the porch, she entered the house and immediately sniffed the aromatic atmosphere. 'What the hell's going on here?' she cussed. She cocked an ear to the music emitting from the relaxation tape.

Such was the distraction of the therapy, Alf and Flora failed to notice Miriam standing in the bedroom doorway. She coughed loudly to gain their attention. Flora looked up, yelped, then stared straight at Miriam. She could not think of anything appropriate to say so said nothing.

Sir Alf looked up at Flora and smiled, as though to say, 'Don't worry.' He raised himself up on his elbows. 'Been there long have you? Seen enough?' he snapped.

'Plenty, but I thought I'd seen everything,' Miriam sniggered.

'It's not what you think,' said Flora, getting upset.

'No?' Miriam questioned.

'It's part of his treatment.'

'For what?' Miriam shouted with a disbelieving laugh. 'To me it looks like you taking advantage of a man with no legs but plenty of cash.'

'You bitch!' Alf growled. He hoisted himself up and swung round until his legs hung over the edge. 'She's done more for me in a couple of months than you did all the years we were married.' He slid off the bed and stood on the floor. 'See this? I'd still be in the bloody chair if it were left to you!' he ranted.

'Dead right you would. See you in court, you and your lady, 'cos you'll be the main witness,' Miriam hissed at Flora.

'Don't mind yourself over her,' Alf reassured Flora. 'This bust-up has been on the cards for a while. Just sorry you had to be here when it happened.'

Flora smiled thinly.

They stood there for a minute, not speaking, just mulling over their predicament. The phone ringing in the hall cut short any verdict. 'I'll get it,' said Flora and dashed off.

Sir Alf pulled on his trousers, and then grinned. 'Day started OK, got even better and then went down the pan. What the hell!'

'Terry Cargill for you.'

'Man must be bloody psychic,' he quipped. With the aid of two crutches, he hobbled into the other bedroom and took the call. 'Just about to call you, you must be a mind reader.'

Terry sounded sombre. 'You've heard then.'

'Heard what?'

'About your Roland. He's being questioned by the police.'

'Him and his bleeding fast cars, I knew they'd get him in trouble.'

'Got nothing to do with fast cars. It's about the club burning down. Serious, this. They found a body, and he's in deep shit, if you ask me.'

'Did I say the day was going down the pan?' Sir Alf muttered. 'I'll meet you at the station, soon as I'm ready. Oh, by the way … I need you to sort out a divorce…'

'All change, eh?' Terry commiserated.

'You don't know half of it,' Alf replied, putting down the phone before he had finished talking.

John's Bad Luck Continues

'Thanks for coming. Don't know anyone else to talk to,' John Appleby confided in Tom Deakin.

'No problem, glad to help.'

They were sitting in the kitchen. As John poured the tea he was physically shaking. 'I'm sure it was meant for me.'

'What was?'

'This prank. It killed the old chap next door this morning. I'm sure it were meant for me.' Tom listened in disbelief. 'Early hours, this awful racket on the door just like last time. Thought I'd get the bastard this time. I tried to open the door but it'd only open a bit. Turns out next door's knockers and mine were tied together. It must have disturbed the old chap next door. He must have tried to open his door and of course it wouldn't. When I tried to open my door, it shut his door, and so on … went on for ages. I could hear him shouting. He must have panicked. No other way out of these back-to-backs. Then it all went quiet. They found him dead behind the door.'

'Frigging hell,' was all Tom could say.

***

Down at *The Throttle Flyer*, Arnold Bosworth was sitting at his desk mulling over a pleasant predicament. 'What do you reckon, Martin?' he asked his sub-editor, who was really just a dogsbody with a posh title. 'Should we go with the cricket club fire or the death of the pensioner at the hands of a prankster?'

The sales of the paper had risen dramatically recently. Arnold, of course, put this down to his hard-hitting, no-nonsense, front-page banner headline. As usual, he decided to go with the most sensational one-liner he could devise.

'*Body found in gutted club… gutted body found in club… clubbed body found in gutted … prank death shocks town…* Nah, too soppy… Got it!' he yelled.

Martin was no longer listening.

'*Who's Next?* Big letters, big question mark. That should put the shits up them. Nice to have something to get me teeth into.'

That afternoon, as the printing press ran at blinding speed to get the paper on the stands, Martin eavesdropped on a conversation Arnold did not appear to enjoy. 'You stupid little shit, I told you not to ring here. A better bike? You must be joking! Look, can't talk here, I'll give you a ring, OK… Don't ever call here again.' With that, he slammed down the phone, looked round and his mind went into overdrive.

Same Police Station,
Different Interviewee

'Mr Bullock, can you account for your petrol-stained trousers being found near the scene of the burnt-out cricket club?' probed the detective.

'No,' Roland responded.

'Did you pour petrol around the club with the intention of–' the detective's question was cut short by the young constable standing to attention.

'Psst, psst...'

'Something wrong, constable?' the detective barked.

'No, sir,' he replied.

'Explain yourself outside.'

The detective followed the constable. Roland sat in silence looking at the door, but he could hear nothing. Ten minutes later, the detective re-entered the room. The red eyes bore witness to the fact that he had eventually got the two-week-old joke, and realised the significance of the motif painted on the works entrance door. 'Shall we continue … Mr – err – Bullock?'

The detective stared at his notes. 'Serious business this. Incendiary device, destruction of property and a fatality – smacks of a good few years in nick. Let me tell you what I think: you were a bit upset about the graffiti on your door, you suspected it were someone at the club, so you blew it up and killed an occupant at the same time. The actions are a bit extreme, I grant you, but revenge and retribution can sometimes get out of hand. So is that how it was?'

If the detective was hoping for a quick solution, he was wrong. 'I was miles away when the club went up. And whoever painted the door must have also stolen my pants and left them there as a set-up.'

The detective gathered his notes and stood up. 'Your money won't get you out of this. I'll see to it that you go down.'

Roland looked at him and sneered. 'Ah, now I recognise you. You're that Harold Whatsisname. I knew you when we were kids. You never did like me, did you?'

***

That afternoon Sir Alf met Terry Cargill in his office. 'Where do we start?' Terry asked.

Sir Alf looked stunned. 'Everything's falling apart,' he muttered, wringing his hands and staring at the floor.

'Let's take it one stage at a time then we're less likely to miss anything,' Terry said reassuringly. 'First, Roland. They seem to have a strong case but it's based on circumstantial evidence. No one actually saw him light a match, even though it looks certain that he poured the petrol under the clubhouse.'

'He'll go down then,' sighed Sir Alf.

'Early days yet; they'll have to prove that he set fire to the club to prove manslaughter. Could be arson or just damage to property. Going to be tricky though.'

'Jesus, manslaughter! Arson! Never thought I'd hear those words.' Sir Alf put his head in his hands.

'About the divorce,' said Terry slightly louder than he intended.

'Been on the cards for years, but being caught out with the hired help kind of put the tin hat on it,' said Sir Alf resignedly.

Terry grinned. 'Not much wrong with you then.' He sat back and straightened his professional face. 'Knowing the lady as I do, and the probable mood she's in, she'll be after half. So what's it to be, the house or the works?'

Sir Alf, shocked, looked up. 'Do I have a choice?'

'Look, I don't know all your financial details … but making an educated guess, I'd say your house must be worth a mint and your lock-up units about the same, maybe more. She'll want half, so which do you want to sell to raise the cash?'

'Simple as that, lifetime's work gone,' Sir Alf sighed.

Terry softened his voice and smiled. 'Look, I know it's a bastard but that's the way it is. Lot of people would want your problem.'

'Give me a day or two, will you? Some serious thinking to do. Can you get me a cab?'

'It could be an awful lot worse,' Terry said with a broad grin. 'There are folk out there who'd love to be in your shoes, especially when it comes to the hired help.'

Sir Alf forced a smile, but did not speak.

'Good to see you're on your feet again, it solves one problem,' Terry added, pointing at Sir Alf's legs.

'Early days yet. They ache like bastards after a while, not sure I can cope with going back to work yet,' Sir Alf said, pursing his lips and gripping his thigh.

'Leave Roland to me. I'll get on to you as soon as I hear anything,' Terry added as Sir Alf hobbled to the door.

Sir Alf clambered into the back of the cab and they set off towards home. As they passed the cricket club, he saw the cordoned-off remains of the building. Two days after the fire, onlookers were still staring at the blackened rubble, hoping to spot something gruesome sticking out from the charred timbers.

'Funny do that,' said the driver.

'Don't see anyone laughing,' Sir Alf snapped.

'I didn't mean it like that. What I was trying to say was, all that fuss over trying to keep the club going, no bugger goes anyway, and now it ends like this. It's like it were meant to be, if you get my drift.'

Sir Alf would have replied but he was mentally calculating the acreage.

He let himself in and flopped into his wheelchair, which was conveniently parked inside the door, then whizzed into the kitchen. He braked hard at the sight of the figure slumped, head on arms, at the breakfast table. 'Flora, didn't expect to find you here!'

'I feel awful about this business with Miriam, really awful,' she said, her voice breaking up.

He moved forward and ruffled her hair. 'Hey, don't you go worrying about this lot. There's lots of folk that wish they were in our position.' He clicked on the kettle then, after a pause, added, 'Apparently.'

Flora, puzzled, looked up and forced a smile through mascara-stained eyes. 'Oh Alf, what are we going to do?'

'Well actually, I thought we could finish off the oil. Is there much left?'

That evening Sir Alf was resting; he felt warm and relaxed and despite all the goings-on, he was OK with the world. He could even feel his legs. 'What a grand lass,' he thought as he reflected on the afternoon's treatment. He smiled as he remembered how they laughed at his remark about making good use of that oil. 'Don't be rude,' she had giggled as she wiped him down with a towel.

He was just drifting off to sleep on the settee when he heard a knock at the front door. 'Bleeding hell's this?' he muttered as he grabbed his crutches then hobbled to answer it. 'Good God!' he shouted as he stared at Benjamin filling the doorway. 'Give somebody a heart attack, doing a thing like that.'

'Sorry Mr … Sir.'

'Alf, just call me Alf.'

'I didn't mean to scare you.'

'Come and talk in the kitchen.'

Benjamin sniffed the air. 'There's a wicked fragrance in here.'

'It's the polish. Cleaner's been today. Now what can I do for you?'

'Your Roland, he's been a badass to the club.'

Sir Alf nodded, 'Aye, aye.'

'Point is, I can get him off the hook but I'm not sure he deserves it.'

Sir Alf looked at him in a way that said, 'I know he's been a badass, but this is my son we are talking about.'

'Really?' he said out loud.

'You see, I saw him leg it across the pitch at least an hour before the club went up.'

'Oh!' Sir Alf responded. 'How did you know it were him?'

'Aren't many dudes round here can afford them expensive boxers. Oh, he left this behind too.' Benjamin held out a leather credit-card holder with RB embossed in gold on the corner.

'Don't you think you should go to the police? They can have you for withholding evidence.'

'Oh, I'll be going, just *when* is the question. You see, those down at the club have been very good to me and I feel I should return the favour. So I've come here to talk man to man about the club's future.'

'Now look, if you think you can blackmail me…' said Sir Alf, losing his temper.

'No, no, nothing like that, more … reassurance, that's all. Keep cool,' Benjamin responded, holding up his hands.

'The only reassurance I can give you at this time is that there will be a decision and it'll be made, let's say, with the village's best interest at heart.'

'Seems fair enough, can't ask for more than that.'

After Benjamin had gone, Sir Alf pondered, 'Well at least it won't be manslaughter … but it was close.' His emotions were mixed. He was glad his only son would be off the major charge. 'But he did pour the petrol under the club and it's more luck than good judgement that he wasn't the one to set it off,' he ranted to the empty house.

About the same time, in the back room of the Ram Inn, 'Sad do, sad do, what an awful waste,' said Simon Jakeson to one of his mates.

'Did anyone know his name?' asked the friend.

'No, no. I'm on about all that ale going to waste. Do you think it could have survived all that heat?'

Decision Time

Susan had recently sensed a change in her mood, her appetite and, more importantly, her monthly cycle. A tester from the local chemist indicated the reason and gave her a problem she could have done without.

'There was always an element of risk,' she said to the mirror as she flushed the remains of the kit down the toilet. 'But I'm afraid continuing is out of the question.'

Later that day, she presented herself at Joe Lagg's front door.

'I'm still sick!' he shouted through the letterbox.

'You'll be more than sick if you don't let me in,' she replied.

'I'm still sick I tell you! Bog off!'

'Do you know what they do to men like you in prison? First, they rape the shit out of them, then they...' Susan heard the various chains and latches being undone.

'What's up for God's sake?' he asked angrily as he closed the door behind them.

A couple of minutes later, he shouted, 'Fifteen hundred quid! What the hell for?'

'Look, I'm not going to beat about the bush. I wouldn't ask if it weren't urgent.'

'Just tell me why I should, that's all. All you've ever done is threaten me.'

'Now look, if you want to join your mate, it can be arranged,' Susan said, wagging a finger at him.

'See … you're threatening me again.'

She grabbed the door handle and turned it as she feigned departure. To her relief, it worked.

'OK, OK … though I don't know why.'

She let go of the handle and smiled. 'It's a favour, doing someone a good turn. You'll feel much, much better afterwards.'

He was recovering from writing the cheque by sipping a strong cup of tea laced with whisky when the doorknocker rattled again. 'Mrs Bullock... Come in, why don't you.'

But Miriam was already down the hall by the time he had said 'in'.

'What the bloody hell are you two up to?'

'Which two?'

'Don't mess me about. I guessed before I went away that you two were putting pressure on the cricket club ... so...'

'Nowt to do with me, I've been in my sick bed for two weeks, ask Susan.'

'Susan? Susan who?'

'Oh ... no one.'

'You're hiding something.'

'I'm not ... it's nowt to do with me, I keep telling you.'

She gripped the top of his towelling robe, along with a good handful of chest hairs. 'You lard arse, you were always soft when you were a kid. Tell me the truth or I'll ... I'll...'

Having been harangued and fleeced out of fifteen hundred quid only moments earlier, and still feeling flu-like, Joe's pain threshold was at an all-time low. He had no option. 'OK ... OK ... it were just a bit of fun.'

Tea Break at *The Throttle Flyer*

Arnold was having a 'no news' day – at least not the type of news he wanted.

'More than you can cope with these days, eh,' Martin said.

Arnold was chewing his pen top along with a cold sausage sandwich. 'Oh,' he muttered, licking some half-chewed bread off the cap of his biro. He pointed the damp end of his pen at Martin and lectured. 'Everyone knows about the fire. No one's interested in some old git snuffing it behind a door, it's ordinary news, everyday ordinary news, it won't sell papers! But smut sells! Dirty goings-on sell papers! What we need is some filth!' he said, spitting sausage across his desk.

Martin threw out a sprat. 'Well, Lord and Lady Muck are splitting up and their lad's in the nick on suspicion of the club fire. It's all over the place.'

'So?' Arnold replied, unimpressed.

This was before Arnold's time, so the newly promoted sub-editor had to fill in the blanks. 'Apparently he's been having it away … they don't know who with…'

'Hang on, hang on, the guy's in a wheelchair, isn't he?'

Martin nodded.

Arnold sat up and with renewed vigour started scribbling headlines. '*Triangle, wheel, degrees, Mill man spins web of deceit.* There's a line here somewhere. I need more info.'

An hour later, he stood at the entrance to Sir Alf's house, pen and pad at the ready. Flora opened the door a fraction and peeped out.

'*Throttle Flyer* here. Would Sir Alfred like to comment on the apparent collapse of his dynasty?' As he spoke, he put his foot in the doorway, a trick that a Fleet Street journalist had taught him. 'While you're talking they don't watch your feet,' he'd been advised. Unfortunately he'd forgotten the other advice: 'Wear stout shoes, not trainers.'

The well-worn trainers were no match for solid oak doors, especially when slammed by Flora, whose arms had been strengthened by hours of massage.

'What's all the commotion?' said Sir Alf, arriving to find the wily reporter holding his crushed foot.

'Says he's got dysentery, wants a comment.'

'What do you want?' Sir Alf shouted down at Arnold as he held his swelling foot.

'An ambulance.'

'Don't know about an ambulance. Hard-boiled eggs used to do the trick, get six of them down you and you'll not shit for weeks.'

Flora looked at the reporter, then Sir Alf. 'Must be severe, look at his face.'

Sir Alf turned and laughed at Flora: 'Well he's got his comment. Can you call him an ambulance, love?'

As the increasing pain racked his leg, a thought zapped Arnold's brain: the word 'love' and the affectionate smile. 'Gotcha...' He smirked for a split second and then the pain took over again.

Hours later, sporting a gleaming white plaster on his ankle, he sipped tea in the Milky Coffee Café while his companion made slurping noises through a plastic straw as he reached the bottom of his milkshake. 'Can I write on it?' Craig asked as he let the straw drop into the glass.

Still in some pain, Arnold was beginning to lose his patience. 'No you bloody well can't. Now concentrate, will you!'

'Want a new, better bike. This one's shite,' Craig sulked.

'You'll get a new bike when you've done the work. Names and times, names and times,' Arnold repeated. 'I want to know who goes where up at the Bullock house, got it?'

'Can I have another milkshake?'

Arnold closed his eyes and held the outside of the plaster cast.

***

The following day, Craig cycled up to the Bullock house.

'Alf … you seen that lad sitting in the bushes?'

'Aye, he's been there a while now. Just sits there. Could do with some lessons in espionage, if that's what he's up to.'

They stared at him through the net curtains; he, in turn, stared back.

'I don't think he's there for the benefit of his health. I'll sneak out of the back while you keep him occupied – better take me stick.'

Flora offered him his stick and held open the back door. 'Keep him occupied how?' she asked.

'Use your initiative,' he added with a dirty grin that she had not seen before.

'You must have a low opinion of me'

He got into his wheelchair and whizzed out around the back of the house. Meanwhile Flora placed a low table at the bedroom window and climbed onto it. She drew back the net curtains and waved at the lad then she started to gyrate. She could see his head nodding to her movements. She mouthed, exaggeratedly and slowly, 'Want to see more?' As she saw the binoculars go up and down, she casually undid the top buttons to her blouse. 'More?' she suggested.

The binoculars moved up and down again. She pulled at her blouse to reveal a portion of cleavage. It was then she saw the top of Sir Alf's head speeding down the lane towards the boy. 'More?' she teased. She leaned forward, her sexy smile changed to a leer, then she pulled out her tongue and raised her middle finger.

The boy dropped his gaze to see Sir Alf racing towards him. He climbed on his bike and set off but the powerful chair swiftly overtook him. As he drew alongside, Sir Alf shoved his walking stick through the front spokes of the cycle wheel. Bike and rider cartwheeled into the grass verge.

Sir Alf edged the chair up against the stricken lad. 'What you up to?' he shouted, raising the stick up in the air.

Back at the house, he related the story to Flora. 'He were snooping for that bloody reporter. It's not funny, you know,' he added, noting Flora's smirk.

'I know it's not, I just enjoyed teasing him, that's all. It's a good job you weren't any longer, I'd have been down to my smalls.'

'If I'd have known that, I'd have hung on a bit.'

'You've changed your tune, must be the fresh air. Apparently it affects men of your age.'

'Is it time for my aromatherapy yet?' Alf grinned as he grabbed her leg.

***

Later that day, top floor at *The Throttle Flyer*. 'Bob! Hello, it's Alf Bullock.'

There was a pause as Bob Riley, non-executive director of *The Throttle Flyer*, cast his mind back. 'Of course … how the hell are you? Bloody hell, it must be years...'

'Aye, that's what everyone says. Beginning to think I've been on another planet.'

'Good to hear from you. We must have a pint.'

'Aye, grand idea, but it's not a social call.'

There was another pause. 'Go on then.'

'It's one of your men, he's been snooping up at the house, or rather, his bleeding lap dog has. I'd appreciate it if he were stopped.'

'Don't tell me, Arnold Bosworth,' Bob sighed.

'Well … aye, least I think it is. Didn't catch his name.'

'You're not the first. Silly bastard will have us in court next. I'll have his wings clipped, if not cut off altogether.'

'You're a gem. We must have that pint.'

After the Fire

'The good news is the beer's OK,' Tom advised as he gulped down most of his pint in one go.

'Like it were meant to be,' added Janice glumly. The committee had borrowed the back room of the pub for a meeting. 'Aye well … life goes on, I suppose.'

'Unless you're one of them there anarchists.'

'Aye, he didn't last long,' Janice said.

Susan had been putting on a brave face since her away day, but her emotions were not one hundred per cent. Not getting a response, Janice repeated her comment, 'No life at all, had he?'

'Sorry, mistake to come,' Susan said through a flood of tears. They watched her disappear through the door.

'Have you been upsetting her?' Tom asked. Janice shook her head. Silence swept through them for a moment then Tom broke the ice. 'Ben's off in a few days. We should show some appreciation.'

The others grinned as John Appleby read their thoughts.

'A karaoke night.'

'A tent.'

'A marquee.'

'A cleaner,' added Janice.

'A meeting!' shouted Arthur Padstow.

***

Arnold was planning his next move. Across the table at the Milky Coffee Café, a somewhat distressed accomplice related the incident with the wheelchair.

Craig held his arm. 'The old git were going to hit me with his stick, had me pinned down with his chair. That were after he wrecked my bike – he put his stick through the wheel. It's knackered now.'

'I only promised you a bike if you got the goods, so what have you got? Come on, what have you got?' Arnold repeated with no concern at all for the boy's health.

'Nothing.'

'All that time … nothing!' growled Arnold. He gripped Craig by the shirt. 'And what did you tell him?'

'Nothing, honest.'

'You lying little shit.' He pulled the boy closer by the lapels. 'If I find that you've…'

The discussion they were having had caused interest, so much so that other customers had tuned in and the proprietor had stopped pouring tea mid-order. Arnold looked round, let go of the lad's lapels and smoothed out the creases.

'A new bike? Of course you can have one. What colour?'

Craig noticed the change in his fortune but then pushed his luck a little too far. 'You'd better, you twat, or I'll tell everyone what you've been up to.'

Arnold rested his aching leg on the rail underneath the table. He contemplated his circumstances for a moment, then leaned forward and whispered, 'Right, yes, new bike, I'll swap it for the old one tonight, but I can't be seen handing it over. Meet me at the viewpoint about half nine.'

Craig hastily got up and rushed out. As he fled through the door, Arnold scanned the menu. 'Should be dark by then,' he muttered.

Having finished his mid-afternoon break, Arnold hobbled back to the office. Martin, who had a silly grin on his face, greeted him. 'Don't sit down, you're wanted, top floor,' he advised.

Arnold laughed. 'Must be another bonus. I wasn't really expecting it till next month.'

'Don't think so,' said Martin.

An hour later, Arnold was sitting in his car in the car park. 'Sacked! Me! The best bleeding reporter they ever had! The little bastard must have run right to them. Well, it's him … then the rest.'

Among the Flowers and Singing Birds

Joe was beginning to feel much better: the antibiotics the doctor had prescribed had eventually worked. He still did not know what the illness was; when the doctor asked, he spoke of hallucinations, fever and delirium. He was finding it difficult to remember the goings-on of the past few weeks. In fact, he was enjoying his break so much that he contemplated total retirement.

'Susan what's-her-name needs a job, she can sodding well have one – mine.'

He leant back on the lounger and sipped his herbal tea. He closed his eyes and felt the warmth of the sun on his face. He listened to a skylark and began to drift. The glass in his hand started to tilt; although he knew it was falling, he could not keep a grip of it. Then curiously, he felt the glass being supported. 'Don't drop your glass, Mr Lagg,' said a gruff but familiar voice.

Panic-stricken, he opened his eyes to find the Jakeson brothers looking down on him, one on either side. Immediately, his heart pounded. 'Heck did you get in here?'

'We tried the front door but got no answer, so we figured you'd be round here.'

The sight of these large gentlemen peering down at him made his breathing go haywire. Panting heavily, he stared upwards. The bright sunlight made him blink uncontrollably; he gripped the top of his dressing gown. 'Fuck do you want?' he screamed.

'About three grand was the figure mentioned, if our memory serves.'

'What?' he screamed again.

The faces came closer. 'You said three grand if the games stopped and they don't get a cup.'

'Well they are and they won't,' said the other brother. The brothers looked at one another. They thought long and hard, nodded agreement, and then carried on. 'When do we get our money?'

'It could be some time. The man with the cash is in jail.'

'No, *you* get the money or we'll do some alterations, cos that's what we do. We're good at alterations, we can start by making this place look like the fucking cricket club. Then we'll alter you.'

The other brother, eager to have a say, chipped in, 'Yeah, like, err, the hunchback of Notre Dame, cos he's ugly.'

The other brother shook his head and then looked at Joe. 'Fancy being ugly, do you?' Joe shook his head. 'Twenty-four hours then.'

As they passed through the gate, Joe started to shake so much that he dropped his glass.

Still in Charge

Susan was slowly coming to terms with what had happened over the past few months. She was staring at the aquarium screensaver on the computer with a cup of coffee gripped between both hands. As the fish went round and round, so did her thoughts: cricket club; house; Benjamin; Geoffrey and Alison. She was unaware of the damage caused by dripping hot coffee onto a keyboard. Luckily a customer she had chosen to ignore advised her, 'It'll never work again.'

The familiar but unexpected voice caused her to spill the remainder of her cup.

'Now it'll definitely never work again,' said Benjamin.

'Benjamin, how are you?'

'Fine … fine, how are you?' he returned the question. 'You ain't been around.'

'Oh, you know, what with the fire and everything … hadn't the heart.'

'I thought I better come round cos there's something weird happening.' As he spoke, there was a confused expression on his face. Susan could have sworn she saw his eyes watering.

'Come in the back, I'll put the kettle on.'

She locked the door and changed the sign to closed then led him into the back office. They pulled their chairs close and sipped coffee.

'Thing is,' said Benjamin with a croak in his voice, 'I've left stacks of clubs in the past but never had the feelings I've got now. I can't sleep. I'm all churned up.' He held her hand and sniffed. 'I've never felt like this before. I'm even off my food and that's not like me.'

Susan smiled and sniffed back a tear, then stroked his face. 'Oh Ben,' she sighed.

Meanwhile Geoffrey was hovering at the locked door, outside the office. He tried cupping his hands and peering through the window. He looked at his watch and squinted through the glass again.

'It clearly says closed when it should be open,' said a voice from behind.

Geoffrey turned to see Joe Lagg. 'Oh … you.'

'Luckily, I have a key,' Joe said, ignoring Geoffrey's sneer.

'Glad to see somebody's lucky.'

'Yes, yes, OK,' said Joe, inserting the key in the door.

'Where's Susan?' Geoffrey asked.

'She should be here and this place should be open.'

They looked at the light coming from under the door of the back room. Susan and Benjamin heard the door being opened and looked at each other.

'They won't understand – hide!' she hissed. When the door opened, she was sitting at Joe's desk holding some papers. 'Oh hello, thought I heard the door.'

'You OK?' asked Geoffrey.

'Oh yes, just thought I'd catch up on some paperwork. It's easier if I just close for ten minutes.'

'We never close,' said Joe curtly.

Geoffrey gripped Joe's arm. 'Well, I think it's a good idea. You'll get fewer disturbances that way.'

'OK, yes, good idea, but I need a key from the drawer.'

Hastily Susan pulled open the drawer and handed Joe a large bunch of keys. 'Here,' she said, raising her voice.

Joe went into the corner, paused and turned. 'Look away,' he instructed, then fumbled with the lock of a large old oak bureau. It matched the desk in size, which was fortunate for Benjamin and his six-feet-six frame as he was crouched in the kneehole.

As they spoke, he felt peculiarly secure; he wrapped his arms around Susan's legs and rested his head on her knees. She leant over the top of the desk and placed her elbows on the blotting pad so that the top of his head would not show. Geoffrey was not used to seeing Susan in this official capacity. He was impressed by the way she sat at the desk, leaning forward, glasses perched on the end of her nose, pen in hand, effectively in charge. So impressed was he that he remained silent, dumbstruck. His imagination was just getting into gear when…

'Geoffrey?' she said, alerting his attention.

He looked round, blinked and tried to respond. 'Yes … oh yes, we've got to go to the school. Alison's been hurt, nothing much, just a graze. They said we might want to take her to the hospital, just to be safe.'

'For God's sake! So why are we dawdling here?'

The noise of Benjamin's head hitting the top of the desk was lost in her abuse of Geoffrey. She ushered both Geoffrey and Joe towards the door. 'Come on!' she hurried, raising her voice. She looked at Joe, who was hesitating. 'Come on! It won't matter if it's shut till tomorrow.'

Once at the threshold, she uttered a cryptic message to Benjamin who was now rubbing his head and having second thoughts about a relationship. 'I'll carry on with this when I come back tomorrow … about nine!' she shouted, apparently to an empty room.

Joe and Geoffrey exchanged puzzled looks but put it down as the ranting of a disturbed woman. They went their separate ways at the door, Geoffrey running behind Susan and Joe clutching a fat manila envelope.

Benjamin waited until the voices faded, then crawled out from under the desk.

'Now that was close,' he said, straightening his clothes. 'But it's going to be a long night.'

***

Craig was sitting on the boulders near the viewpoint. He was sweating after pushing the twisted bike all the way up the hill. The real part he hated was the constant ribbing from people he met on the way. They laughed, pointed and gave him all kinds of advice on the correct way of riding it. Now he was here with his bike but the other person was not. He looked repeatedly at his watch.

'He said half nine,' he muttered.

In fact, Arnold was close by in his car in a lay-by. He also looked at his watch. 'Shit! It's still light. I'll give it another ten minutes,' he grumbled.

It was ten o'clock before he thought it dark enough to make a move. Craig, however, had decided to call it quits and was on his way down by then.

Arnold raced up the hill and caught Craig in his headlights. 'Got you, you little shit!' he shouted as he veered across the road. 'Grass me up with my boss, would you!'

At first Craig was not aware that he had become a target; he just stepped back a bit from the road. Then, as the car came straight for him, he let go of his bike and started to run back up the hill. He heard a crunch and a scraping noise as the car went over the bike; he paused for a fraction of a second and thought he recognised Arnold's wild eyes staring through the windscreen.

Arnold did not pause. The accelerating car hoisted Craig over the bonnet and across the windscreen. Arnold wrenched at the steering wheel in an attempt to shake Craig off the car. With the lad obscuring his view, he drove off the road and down the steep grassy embankment. He hung on to the wheel as the car ripped through deep bracken. Then, with a mighty bang, it halted as it hit a track to a farmhouse.

Arnold awoke a few hours later cold, sore and very damp. He gripped the steering wheel as if the car were still moving then, as realisation set in, he looked around. The ignition and lights were still on. The windscreen was cracked – he was not sure if he had done it or Craig, but his head ached like crazy. He looked at his watch; it was just after midnight. He tried the engine and it spluttered into life but it was strangely loud. 'Fucking exhaust,' he cursed. He pressed the clutch with his good foot, tried to put the car in gear and then yelped, 'Jesus, what have I done?'

He tried again, this time using both hands. He edged the car forward to straighten it up and reversed back along the track. As it swung round, the headlights picked out a shape in the bracken. He knew what it was and ignored it. Gingerly, and as quietly as he could, he reversed along the track and back onto the road. As he drove up the hill he spotted the remains of the bike: it still had sections of gleaming new paint but its shape was that of a banana.

Arnold got out of the car and limped towards the bike. Everything hurt and his trousers stuck to him. He looked down in disgust then dragged the bike onto the road as best he could and sent it down the hill. 'Here's your bike, you little shit!'

He climbed back into the car and slowly drove home, trying not to rev the engine for fear of alerting unwanted attention. He locked the car in the garage and hobbled into the house. As he put the bolt on the door, he spluttered, 'That's one done, then.'

Does Anyone Know?

It was a good few days before Arnold dared venture out. Finally, the lack of basic sustenance and the desire to scour *The Throttle Flyer* got the better of him.

The swelling had receded in his hand and, with the help of a bottle of pills, his headache had also gone. He hobbled round to the garage and opened the up-and-over door.

'Jesus!' he exclaimed as he saw the wreck that used to be his car. 'If I go out in this, I'm dead.'

He slammed down the door and, after retrieving the aluminium crutch the hospital had lent him, set off to the shop. It was curious, he thought, that when you wanted to be incognito, everyone noticed you and when you were feeling in need of human contact, nobody did. The man in the newsagents who normally would not give Arnold the time of day suddenly wanted to talk.

'How'd you do that?' he asked, pointing to the plastered ankle. 'And that?' pointing to the brightly coloured bruise on his forehead.

'Oh … just … just give me a *Flyer.*'

'Buying one, what for? You writes 'em, don't you?'

Arnold looked away for a moment, disdain for the man clearly showing. 'Look, are you going to sell me one or what?' As he spoke, the pressure increased in his head and immediately the headache returned. He held his head with one hand and his crutch with the other. He thought the plastic clip on the crutch would stay secured to his arm, but no – as he rummaged for change, the crutch clattered to the floor. The vendor added to his predicament by holding out the rolled-up paper.

'God's sake,' Arnold hissed. Unable to stand unaided, he rested on the counter, panting. He reached down for his crutch but it was too far away. An old lady in the queue picked it up and held it out to him. He nodded and then resented the thought of a pensioner helping him.

'Get off, I can manage!' he snapped. But he couldn't, he hadn't enough hands, so he just tipped out a pile of loose change, snatched the paper and shuffled out.

'Ungrateful git,' said the lady.

Unable to wait until he got home, Arnold leant against a wall and scoured the paper for news of the other night. He flicked the pages impatiently until he got to the back page: *Mystery Hit and Run* ran the headline. 'Boring banner,' he muttered.

He skimmed the contents until he got right to the end, then: *A police representative said that although they have no idea about the car or the identity of the driver, the vehicle would be considerably damaged and the driver would have sustained injuries.*

He was mulling over the possible sequence of events when he started to race back through the paper. 'Yes!' he shouted as he spotted a large advert: *Farewell Party for Club Pro – All Welcome.*

Tea Time at the Perkins' House

'Are we going to the do on Saturday?' asked Geoffrey.

'Not keen,' replied Susan.

'Oh come on, we're supplying the beer. A new one – Winter Wonderland it's called.'

'But it's summer.'

'Aye well, we have to try them out. It might as well be on this shower.'

'That's not very nice. These people are your neighbours.'

'Yeah, I know, but I still feel like a bleeding stranger.'

'You get on well with Albert.'

'Oh thanks. Mr Happy, as he's better known.'

Susan moved over to the sink and her mind started to drift. Her mind and her internals were back to where they were a few months before. In her thoughts, she was reluctant to rehash it all again. 'But it was exciting: plots, intrigue, subterfuge plus a bit on the side,' she mulled.

'Well are we going or what?'

'I don't know. You take Albert, it'll be good for him.'

Geoffrey went over and put his arm round Susan's waist. 'You did look well the other day, sitting behind that desk, all officious. Never seen you look like that. It's a good job what's-his-face was there or I'd have been round that desk like a shot.'

For a split second, Susan's mind raced through the possibilities. 'Good job you didn't,' she croaked.

***

As their last duty, the committee met to discuss the leaving do for Benjamin. They sat around two tables pulled together in the pub.

John Appleby's posture stiffened. 'As this is the last formal meeting, I presume we can dispense with the official procedure.'

The others breathed a sigh of relief but as John stood up and held out a paper, they knew he was going to have the last word. 'If I can just … I've written a little farewell speech.'

'God's sake, save it for the leaving do!' they urged.

Tom had other details on his mind. 'What a do! Free beer, booze till it runs out, and no cleaning up afterwards,' he said mockingly, pointing at Janice. 'Fancy tent as well.'

'Do you mind? It's a marquee!' Janice pulled him up.

'Whatever, let's go out with a bang.' The others winced at his unfortunate comment, but did not rise to the bait.

As the committee continued with the preparations for the farewell party, a woman who should have been familiar to them approached, accompanied by a gentleman sporting a healthy tan.

'Sorry to interrupt. They said I could find you here – mind you, nowhere else to go, is there?'

'Miriam, it's Miriam, Alf Bullock's wife,' announced John Appleby. 'God, it must be years,' he added.

'Aye well, wish it were happier circumstances.'

'Can I get you a drink?' offered Fred.

'That would be most welcome. A glass of red, and one for my friend here.'

As the drinks were being poured, the others introduced themselves. Miriam smiled thinly, took a long mouthful of her drink, and then carried on. 'As I said, I believe things have been getting a bit out of control round here. I'm afraid that, for the immediate future, the situation is not clear.'

The others kept quiet as Miriam finished her glass. 'My husband Alf has buggered off to a retreat accompanied by the cleaner – you might know her, local girl half his age called Flora. Roland, my son who sorted your ten-year rule, is on bail for manslaughter so he's not in control any longer. He was supposed to run Bullock Units as a business and make a profit, but he hasn't. So, as you can see, we have a financial conundrum. Well, I'm sorry but the decision has been made to turn the cricket club land over for house building. I really am sorry, I know how you have tried to make a go of it.'

The committee members looked at one another and smiled.

Tom stood up. 'Let me get you another glass of wine.'

'As you can see, we are not exactly upset by your news. In fact, we are quite relieved. It's been a horrible year,' added Janice.

Susan Perkins held up her glass and announced, 'Our house has just gone up ten grand and we can sell it.'

***

The whole village turned up for the leaving do.

'What about me speech?' John said, his voice lost in the din of music. 'Better get out there before it's too late.' He climbed up onto the makeshift stage and, without asking Benjamin who was busy 'mixing', he grabbed the microphone.

'He never learns,' Tom shouted to the others.

John tapped the microphone in time-honoured tradition, and then blew on it. 'Can we 'ave some hush for a minute?' It took ages for the revellers to quieten down. 'Just want to say, we did our best, but as you can see events, conspired against us...' He paused as the events of the last few months flashed by but patience was not a quality used to describe Throttle residents, and muttering started. He continued hastily, 'Aye, it's thanks to Benjamin here and the lads for giving it their best shot. Glad to see so many people have turned up. Maybe we should just organise leaving dos.'

'Stuff that,' added Tom quietly but with feeling.

'So it's thanks to all of you,' John said. The music and dancing started the split second he said 'Thanks', leaving him stranded on the stage holding the microphone. As he clambered down with it still in his hand, it boomed loudly every time he hit the floor.

Meanwhile Arnold had been festering in his flat behind closed curtains. No invite had dropped through his door and he took it personally; despite nobody else getting one, he still felt left out. His boss had done some investigating into Arnold's news-generating antics and had made it known that he was not welcome back. Then the police had knocked on his front door, but he sat on the floor behind it and held his breath.

'We'll call again,' he heard the constable say to his colleague. 'Next time, we'll bring a sledgehammer.' They clearly knew he was in.

Melancholia set in. Arnold opened the cupboard and found a bottle of last year's sherry. He slumped down and poured a tumblerful. Three tumblers later, after he had chucked up, he had hatched a plan to 'wipe out the whole frigging village in one go'.

Most of the villagers were in the marquee, so nobody saw Arnold's bedraggled, bruised and limping figure as he crept around the burnt-out remains of the clubhouse. After prising off the lock, he entered the old store. He struggled to see what he was doing in the dim light so he decided to push open the doors. Between moonlight and streetlight, he could just make out the contour of the diesel ground roller.

He had seen the machine started before during a tea interval, but never done it himself. 'Can't be that bleeding difficult. Now what did the old git do?' he muttered.

Arnold felt for a lever on top of the engine and pushed it forward, turned on the fuel and took hold of the clumsy starting handle. His eyes adjusted to the dark so he could now make out the hole in the front cover where it should go. He braced himself, applied pressure and was surprised at how easily the handle rotated. Faster and faster it turned, without a murmur. Then he recalled the next move. He threw the lever back – but nothing happened. In the dying moment before it stopped turning, black soot belched from the pepper-pot exhaust, accompanied by a deafening noise as the motor burst into life. Arnold felt his hair stand on end.

He hoisted himself aboard and gripped the steering wheel. He could see the silhouette of the revellers against the canvas sides of the marquee. 'An easy target,' he thought.

His excitement heightened as he pushed the gear lever forward. The machine lurched then slowly trundled out of the shed. He waved his arms hysterically as he moved towards the twinkling light of the disco. He had it in his mind that it would be swift, like science fiction, that he would zoom across the pitch and destroy all within, then peel away into the distance. But as the roller chugged at its maximum two miles per hour, Arnold had time to consider his actions. Certainly he would kill them all but a roller is hardly a getaway car and he could hardly walk, let alone run. He quickly counted heads dancing in the tent. 'At least twenty. Life for each one. I'll be banged up forever.'

He squinted and could see the front page: *Key Thrown Away, Killer Locked Up*.

The closer he got, the more he realised what a mistake it would be. Still under the illusion that he was in control of anything but a 1949 ex-war-department road roller, he swung on the steering wheel and applied the brake. Expecting an instant response, he was distressed to feel only a slight drift to the right and not a screeching, swerving halt. This put him on a direct course for the source of electrical power for the event: a small generator loaned by the pub.

The roller hardly stuttered as it buried the generator deep in the soft turf. What little illumination there was immediately disappeared, plunging the marquee into total darkness. The disco, also powered by the generator, wound down to total silence. The revellers paused momentarily as they heard the throb of the approaching roller, and screamed as they fled out of the tent.

The roller ploughed on through the back of the now-empty tent and over the disco equipment. The canvas wrapped itself around Arnold, who was in a blind panic with his foot firmly pressed down on the accelerator in an effort to escape. The bystanders could only watch helplessly as the roller continued across the pitch, wrapped in canvas.

Whether Arnold suffocated prior to being dragged over the top of the roller and buried in the pitch, the coroner could not say. All he did say was, 'It would have been a blessing if he had suffocated because it must have been a slow, grisly death.'

***

Newly promoted, Martin was sitting at his desk. 'What do you think, Roger?' he asked with an air of superiority to his new assistant. '*Cursed Club Claims Another Victim* or *Nut Rolled And Crushed*.' He leaned back on his chair. 'It's there somewhere.'

His new assistant offered little support.

Martin put down his pencil. 'It's what Arnold would have wanted…'

About the Author

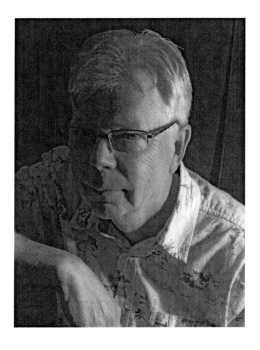

Colin Goodwin enjoyed a successful career as a welding and fabrication engineer, working for the past twenty years in further education, where he also taught stained glass window making.

Recently retired, he is continuing to indulge his creative side by repairing anything mechanical (motor bikes, cars, model steam engines) and is working on the sequel to *Don't Get Mad Get Even*. Colin lives in Lancashire.

Lightning Source UK Ltd.
Milton Keynes UK
UKOW04f1029210715

255553UK00001B/8/P